1976

Mrs. Knox's Profession

By the same author:

A Charitable End

Mrs. Knox's Profession

◇◇◇◇◇◇◇◇◇◇◇◇◇◇◇◇◇◇◇◇◇

Jessica Mann

David McKay Company, Inc.
Ives Washburn, Inc.
New York

MRS. KNOX'S PROFESSION

First American Edition, 1972

LIBRARY OF CONGRESS CATALOG CARD NUMBER: 72-87026

MANUFACTURED IN THE UNITED STATES OF AMERICA

I

The baby clinic only opened once a fortnight, and there were always queues. It was a good day for the regulars to go to the public library next door; they found unfamiliar books appearing on the shelves, marked with return dates long overdue.

Outside the clinic the perambulators stood in rows under a corrugated glass cover. The mothers would carry the babies into the clinic and afterwards leave them tucked in their prams while they did their other local errands. It was reckoned to be a safe place. Passers-by would glance at the prams and sometimes give quick up and down appraisals to the mothers. One of the regular attenders at such clinics thought that it was a sign of her age, that so many of the mothers looked too young to be out of school uniform, like policemen; but some looked so unattractive that she could not think how they had ever had the chance to become pregnant.

The pram was indistinguishable from half a dozen others as she wheeled it away, and so was she from as many of the mothers; chain-store clothes, headscarf and dark glasses, the uniform of a classless society. The baby was asleep, its tiny head concealed under the thick quilt. The day was chilly, though bright. She walked briskly around to the car park at the back of the row of supermarkets, and waited while one of the porters loaded another woman's Mini full of cardboard boxes. Then she opened the back doors of her own estate car, and lifted the baby smoothly into the carrycot which was on the floor. She did everything with an air of such confidence that even when she drove away, leaving the high white pram carelessly behind a delivery lorry, it would have taken an observer a moment to realize that there had been anything unusual about her action. But there had been no observers.

5

Nor was there anybody nearby, for the moment, when a young woman came out of the library with an armful of fiction and strolled along admiring the babies and the elegance of the waiting prams. But a crowd gathered quickly when she started to scream, and her hysteria spread from the wakened babies to their horrified mothers before a soothing policewoman could take her away. However, there was nobody who had seen anything unusual. It was as though the baby's abductor had been invisible.

II

Gordon Buddle's eye fell on the paragraph about the singing star's baby being kidnapped as he laid the folded paper on his master's breakfast table, but he did not take much notice; what did they expect after so much cheap publicity about bringing it up like ordinary people, not splashing their money around, and all that? They shouldn't have taken the baby to the free clinic in the first place. If you had money you should spend it.

He peered closely at the pile of letters, feeling the fatter ones and holding the others up to the light, but none of them revealed anything and he put them in a size-graded pile beside the paper. The bottom one was a bank statement; he'd get a look at that later. He glanced professionally around; coffee on the hot-plate, bacon and eggs under their silver cover, bread ready in the toaster. It was all as it should be and Buddle rather regretted wasting his professional competence on somebody who probably didn't recognize it. He went downstairs for his own second breakfast when he heard the water running out of the bath. He had laid the kitchen table equally neatly for himself, and he sat down to an excellent meal, making approving murmurs as he read his ultra-right-wing paper.

Upstairs, Victor Nightingale read his paper with a closer personal interest. He made a habit of fitting the news to his needs, and kept a pad handy to jot down ideas, off the top of his head, as he liked to call it. It was the same technique which he had successfully used in exams when, even if he could not answer the questions as set, the smart man should be able to twist and adjust so that the knowledge he could display seemed relevant.

It was all about abroad today, and Vic, like those he represented, did not give a damn about foreign affairs. Nor were a flood in the West Country and another kidnapped baby very helpful items of local news. Vic was going to make a corner in housing, and the quality of life, which he had long since worked out would be closest to the hearts of his constituents.

There was a picture of Vic on the middle page, arriving at a function, and he was pleased to see that the photograph showed Folly Armitage smiling at him with apparent intimacy. Cameras never did him justice but with luck people would realize that he must be attractive if a girl like Folly looked at him like that. The picture on his election manifesto was a bit skeletal too, and when he was canvassing nobody recognized him from it, but it did not seem to matter. Face to face he could charm the birds off trees, as his agent complacently remarked.

He turned to his letters with optimism as always, since life was treating him well these days. Nothing from his chief supporter, unfortunately, but the lunch-time post might bring something. It was an effort to make himself open the bank statement and his forebodings were justified. They didn't usually write their polite notes to MPs, but he'd be getting worse than polite notes if this went on. Why the hell was he so broke? He needed more money, and would have to do something about it.

Oh well, not to worry. Something would turn up, as it always did, and he had better not frown any more. There were ominous parallel cracks between his eyebrows in a harsh light already, and eternal youthfulness was part of his image. The old bags down in the constituency would eat him alive if they could. He sighed as he thought of his surgery down there this evening, the most boring and tiresome chore, but the agent insisted on it. He wouldn't go down until the last moment.

Vic Nightingale sighed again, and pushed his chair back from the table. He saw Esmond Smith of the *Daily Perceiver* turning into the street, and walked quickly out for his hat and umbrella. It never did any harm to have informal chats with journalists, and he could make good use of the walk from here up to Sloane Square Underground station.

'Get a case ready, and collect the car, will you, Buddle?' he called down the stairs. 'I'm going down to the constituency this afternoon,' and he let himself out of the house just at the right moment to express surprise and gratification at meeting Esmond Smith.

Buddle came upstairs again when he heard the door slam, and sat down at the shining oval table and poured himself another cup of coffee. He picked up the pile of gutted envelopes and threw it in the wastepaper basket, and then settled down to look at the letters. He had made a habit of reading all he could find for so long that he had almost forgotten that it was not his right to do so. But it was a dull collection today, nothing useful for him; though it was interesting to see just how much in the red the young master was. Where did the cash come from? Buddle had wondered about that the past few months, and was no nearer an answer, though he was reminded by the statement before him now that there had been these lump sums paid in. Unfortunately the computered hieroglyphics gave no indication of their source.

Buddle alone was paid, in a year, a good deal of what Victor Nightingale earned as a member of Parliament, not to mention the perks. And then there was the house in Chelsea, the car, the clothes, the jolly jaunts. This kind of life was not exactly cheap. And yet there were no signs of Vic earning from any other sources, for he was the wrong political colour to be pulling in fat director's fees, and his family had been poor. At least, according to his election handouts he had been to the Ferraby Grammar, which didn't sound as though he had inherited wealth. Why, Buddle thought, his own background was more prosperous

8

than that, for he had been to a minor public school.

Buddle was a realist. When he had left school with mediocre A-levels and the prospect of a lifetime behind a desk, he had felt melodramatically suicidal.

Then one day he was sitting in Hyde Park, and had listened to a couple of nannies talking about their pay.

'I'm getting fifteen, what about you?'

'Oh, eighteen, actually, and the use of the car. And I wouldn't do it without the private bath, would you? I don't fancy sharing.'

'It would be twenty and a private sitting-room if I'd had a year's training,' said the first girl, enviously. 'That Jean, sitting over there with the two kids in orange, she got her boy-friend's mum to write her references and she's getting twenty and three months in Bermuda every year. She hates the job though, says the kids get on her nerves. She was even thinking of going into an office.'

'Go on, never! She couldn't afford it – paying for her own keep, and a flat, and all. And think of having to go out every morning in the rush hour. I look out of the window sometimes, when the kids have gone off to nursery school with the chauffeur and there's me just having a comfortable breakfast, and I look at those girls hurrying to work and think they're crazy.'

Since the part of office life which most deterred Gordon Buddle was the prospect of getting up early and rushing for trains, this comment hit home. He edged around to see the girl who had made it, but she had spots and buck teeth. However, though he abandoned his plans concerning her, thinking that all these girls with wigs deceived a chap – you couldn't tell from behind – the next day he went to a domestic employment agency and was launched on his new career. His mother thought he was a sales representative.

And he was good at his job, what's more. Even as a child he had enjoyed cooking with his mother and helping her with the less tedious bits of housework. He took a professional pride in making sure that the temporaries from the contract cleaners made a good job of the housework, and he was always ready to send back to the shop any food which did not meet his exacting requirements. He knew all about the niceties of brewing coffee and serving wine; more than Vic did, come to that.

He went up to make the bed, and brush yesterday's suit, which he did conscientiously, turning the pockets out and the turn-ups down.

He was hissing through his teeth, the pop music of the nineteen-thirties. Very unrevealing pockets, no receipts or letters. It said in *Who's Who* that Vic had been a journalist. Did journalists make a pile, in a few years? Buddle thought not, and so, apparently, did Buddle's secondary employers.

He moved over to the dressing-table and began to comb the hairs out of the brushes. He'd be bald soon, would our young hero. Buddle wondered about his other employers; what would they get paid for his information? He'd got a cool thousand from his last job for them, finding a handle for poor Champernowne, who had been the opinionated editor of an influential paper. Retired, he had; gone to live in the Cotswolds. The first notch on Gordon Buddle's blade. He carefully avoided thinking about the final destination of the information he dredged up. When he had been recruited he hadn't asked, and it would be better not even to wonder. Anyway, there were plenty of perfectly patriotic people who needed carrots or sticks for British politicians and business men. Could even be the British secret service itself. He, Buddle, might be an unsung British hero. There was no reason to suppose that it was – well, foreigners. Anyway, Handles Ltd, an agency which bought and sold the sort of secrets prominent people would rather not have published, had offered him a lot for this job, so he'd better come up with something.

He opened the wardrobe door and started to make a second check on all the other suit pockets. Surely something must turn up. The trouble was that nowadays so many rules had been relaxed. Twenty years ago there were far more potential levers; homosexuality, for instance. Not that Vic Nightingale was one, but even if he were he would hardly have to conceal it. But there were several female pushovers, who crept in when they thought Buddle wouldn't hear, and

Felicity Armitage didn't try to conceal her presence at all. The way she scattered her belongings – a few years ago it would have been a fiver slipped into his hand for every handkerchief he found crumpled under the pillow and handed back to her, washed and ironed, with his poker face on. These days girls were so careless it did not seem to occur to her that she should be embarrassed about it. She even kept spare make-up round the bathroom. Must be on the pill, though. No bits of rubber to be found, though he had looked.

Buddle sat down in the bedroom armchair with a cigarette to help him consider the problem of his employer's girlfriend. She was pretty enough to be thought brainless, but he did not think that she was nicknamed Folly because she was foolish. There had been some pretty sharp glances at him once or twice, come to think of it. He reminded himself to keep an eye on that girl, and, shuddering slightly, wondered whether she might be interested in him. The other one was just a furtive bit of fun, married, and probably with children. Our Vic would never risk his puritan constituents' reaction to a divorce. Though she might be some use. Buddle doubted whether he quite dared to tackle Miss Armitage about the sources of Vic Nightingale's income, but it might be possible to edge the other one round to the subject. Considering strategy, he went down for his elevenses: whisky and soda, from the drawing-room. It was a comfortable enough life, if nothing else.

As a matter of fact, as well as arranging that it should be comfortable, fate seemed to have decided that his life should work out according to plan. The very next day, after his routine examination of the suit pockets and desk drawers, and some perfunctory housework, since the charwoman did not come that day, Buddle cooked himself an exquisite lunch and ate it in comfort in the dining-room; he was angry with Vic for not giving him longer notice that he would be out; one could have invited a friend to lunch in peace. He was drinking the end of a half-bottle of Moselle, wondering about the money again, and thinking that it could not be the first illegal source which would spring to a

11

layman's mind. After all, if Vic were selling information, then Buddle would not himself have been retained to find it out. That was an idea which he shied away from, since it embarrassed him to think about his second employers' motives and identity. He hastily turned his mind to the thought of his own comfortingly black bank statement. He was building up a nice little nest egg.

Buddle was just thinking of going out, admiring his own man-about-town reflection in the glass above the mantelpiece, when he had to answer the door bell to find Felicity Armitage standing there.

'He's out, is he?' she said. 'Then I'll come in.' She walked past him into the drawing-room, and said, 'Are you just having a drink? I'll join you. I had a rotten lunch.' She sat down at the uncleared table and sipped brandy as he poured himself another glass.

'This is a little unusual, miss,' Buddle said woodenly, but he allowed himself to give her what he thought of as 'the look'.

'Yes, isn't it?' she agreed. 'Where is Vic, anyway?'

'Should be in the constituency.'

'Oh, well, out of the way. Earning his pay, I suppose?'

'A fraction of it,' Buddle said noncommittally.

'Let's hope he has time for some unpolitical earning too,' she said. 'I came to borrow some money. What's the state of his pocket right now?'

Buddle was badly startled by this approach. 'I'm sure I don't know,' he said stiffly.

'Oh, balls. I dare say you know down to the last two pence. What did his bank statement say last time?'

'I —'

'For God's sake, don't pretend you didn't look.'

'Well – he's quite a bit overdrawn, I think.'

'Oh hell. Really? Just when I need some.'

'I'm sorry I can't help you, madam.'

Folly blew a series of smoke rings across the table and looked through them at the embarrassed man. She said:

'Where does he get it anyway? Have you ever seen him do any work?'

12

He hesitated, and decided to plunge.

'Just what I'd like to know. He's had a big lump sum not long ago, paid in cash to his account. And he used to keep some wadges of notes in his desk, but there haven't been any for a while. I've no idea where it comes from.'

'He told me he'd won a premium bond.'

'I don't think he invested it, if that's so,' Buddle said. It might be worth letting this girl in on what he had found out in the hope she had some other pieces of the jigsaw puzzle. 'He doesn't get those glossy circulars which companies send to their shareholders. Anyway, he told me it was a win on the pools.'

'What d'you know about his background – what's your first name, by the way? And give me some more brandy.'

'Certainly. And my name's Gordon. Provincial grammar school, midland redbrick university, ran the place through the student's union. Real little ball of fire he must have been. Organized all their extra-mural activities, went around buttering-up all the citizens, and got himself elected as a surprise the next year. Must have hypnotized the selection committee. And then they were proud as anything to have the youngest MP of the century and all that. They think the sun shines out of his eyes down there.'

'Yes, well, none of that sounds very lucrative. Is he getting a fat retainer from some pressure group, perhaps?'

'I thought of that too. But he must be spending thousands a year that the tax man doesn't know about. I shouldn't have thought he'd be worth that on his back bench.'

Folly Armitage got up and started wandering around the room, looking into cupboards and drawers with casual interest. Somehow it didn't look like snooping when she was so unfurtive, and Buddle reminded himself to change his own technique in future. She put a pop record on and stood jiggling to it on the vibrating floor. She shouted above it:

'He can't be making that honestly.'

Buddle said:

'I don't think he has time for a life of crime. Not burglary or some such, at any rate. I suppose it could be drugs; or blackmail. He could store drugs in his locker at the House and nobody ever the wiser. Safest place in the country. But I've tried probing him about where to get hold of some stuff and he never batted an eye.'

'Oh, he's too pious for that,' shouted Folly, winking her golden eyelid. She went on dancing till the record ended, clicking her fingers with her head thrown back, and bony pelvis jutting forwards. Gordon Buddle watched her intently; the performance, after all, must be for his benefit. She had long loose hair, slightly curly and pinkish blonde; her clothes appeared to have been extracted from some deep recess of her mother's wardrobe, vintage just about the time of her own birth. Her lips were shiny and brightly coloured.

When she stopped dancing she came and sat down beside Buddle, who looked gravely at her.

'I thought I might marry him, if he can afford me,' she said.

'My felicitations, madam,' he replied.

'But he won't tell me whether he can. He just says, "Don't I live in the style to which you're accustomed, then?", and the trouble is that he does. Only I want to be sure he can keep it up.' She laid her hand, crimson-nailed, on Buddle's knee, and moved it gently and suggestively upwards. 'What do you think?'

She looked like an amateur vamp in a war film, he thought. He found the heavy make-up repellent. He was a successful bisexual, himself, and was in the habit of congratulating himself on his catholicity of taste. But the only sort of girls he could take – and given the choice, he preferred boys – were small-breasted, short-haired and not unlike prep school boys. It sent him wild if they had bitten, dirty nails, with inkstained fingers. London was marvellous these days. You could get anything you wanted. But how to get rid of what you didn't want? He calculated rapidly as her greasy lips drew nearer his face and the ugly talons higher on his thigh. A bit too late to pretend to be the loyal servant. And if she did marry the man, she'd come in very nice and useful as a handle; just what was needed, in fact. But was it worth that money to him? He thought of the sum that had been mentioned as his flesh started and chilled with disgust. No, even for that money —

He stood up sharply.

'Thanks ever so,' he said, his voice an octave higher than usual. He turned his toes and hands outwards and pushed his hips forward. Simpering slightly, to make himself absolutely clear, he murmured:

'I'm afraid you've made a mistake.'

She dropped her hand at once, apparently unoffended. 'Sorry,' she said. She took out her compact and reddened her mouth still more. 'No offence meant.'

'And none taken, I'm sure,' he answered primly.

'But I still want to find out about Vic's cash,' she said.

'May I ask why?'

'My papa isn't keen, unless he knows about it all. He still thinks in terms of settlements, and all that. He lives about fifty years ago, poor old thing. But I want him to agree.'

'It isn't – er – necessary, surely?'

'No, I'm twenty-five. But Vic won't want me without family approval. It's not just me, it's the Armitages he needs.'

'You don't seem to mind.'

'Well, I'm realistic. And I want Vic anyway. But I won't get him unless I can lay on the family tiara and the odd seat on a family board. And I can't produce all that unless the family gets Vic's credentials. Not his family and all that. They wouldn't dare go on about ancestors even if they are old-fashioned. But they'll want to know where the money comes from. It matters, you know?'

Gordon Buddle nodded. The pedigree of money could well matter. He was intending to manufacture a positively heraldic one for his own, once amassed. Which reminded him that his aim was the same as hers, if the motives were different.

'I suppose there are always private detectives,' she said. 'But it's a bit embarrassing.'

'I think we ought to manage between us.' He smiled, his fleshy lips exposing flawless teeth. 'It's just a matter of

15

organization. You'll tell me if you do find out anything, will you?'

'I suppose that would be fair, if you'll do the same for me.' She looked at him incuriously.

'You don't mind? After all – if you're going to be Mrs N., you might.' He felt that before exerting himself in the least on her behalf he must find out whether it was worth while. But she'd be a useful ally one day, if kept sweet. Not one to take umbrage, anyway, thank goodness. He thought for a moment of the elder Champernowne daughter, screaming like one of the peacocks on her father's terrace when he'd offered her a little nest egg.

'I never care why people do things,' she said flatly. 'Life's too short. I'm interested in awfully few people, me, mostly. So long as I'm all right, Jack ... But just now I want something else as well.'

She didn't look as hard-boiled as she liked to make herself out, he thought. There'd be handles for Folly waiting to be unearthed, he had no doubt. But first things first. He stood up to help her with her chair, and opened the front door for her as he had been trained to do. He bowed from the shoulders as he said 'Good day, madam.' It was only after she had gone that he noticed that he was hardly dressed like a butler. It spoiled some of his recurrent pride in the perfection of his performance.

III

Knowing that one was neurotic did not make it possible to stop being governed by unreasonable compulsions and fears; Sylvia White had decided this long since and no longer tried to rise above her obsessions. Some were relatively acceptable to the world, in any case, for widows were expected to devote their affections to pet animals and her long-haired Persians were so adorable that nobody could so much as raise an eyebrow at them. It was more inconvenient to need absolute quiet, and the fact that this was vital to her had forced Mrs White to move house three times since her husband died. Sebastian, having spent his youth at boarding-schools and holiday camps, since he was a robust and undecorative boy, was now investigating the atom in the American Middle West, and it was safe for his mother to bemoan her loneliness to her friends without fear that her son would feel obliged to take practical steps to assuage it.

Mrs White had lived in Weston Grange Road for a couple of years now, and she really felt that this was home; the house was well detached from its neighbours, and with the wooden floors carpeted and the walls covered in hessian, harsh sounds were effectively muffled. She was able to escape the milkman and his whistling by sleeping at the back of the house; her bedroom backed on to the garden, and she could not even hear the hum of traffic from the main road.

At the shop, where she sold the relics of a more gracious past, her ears were perpetually assailed by the modern world. It was a ground floor and basement in a busy shopping alley, and huge lorries were always squeezing through, almost scraping the parked cars and the plate-glass windows. So she really needed her oasis of peace. It was vital to her sanity, and she felt that she had the right to expect a little consideration. After all, one would never have bought the house if one had not been assured of its tranquillity and silence.

The houses were expensive, for it was a very desirable district of Orton, and when Mrs White moved in most of the other residents were elderly people who had retired to live on their golden handshakes. It was rather a blow when she found they were dying off, and young families with noisy children were moving in. Fortunately, so far, old Mrs Todd and her equally aged housekeeper in the house on the left, were surviving, and the only disturbance was when a tottering gardener pushed the motor-mower up and down the flawless lawn twice a week. The house on the other side belonged to a middle-aged and childless couple who had recently moved there. Mrs White felt that one might have relied on them to be sober and quiet, especially since the husband was away all the week. She supposed that he was a rather superior version of a commercial traveller.

It was not surprising, therefore, that Mrs White should have felt that her neighbour was getting at her personally, that the offence was an intolerable insult, when the noises from next door disturbed her evenings. Why, she could actually hear the baby crying from inside her house! It was outrageous that she should be expected to listen to such a wailing and caterwauling. Not that her own darlings ever made noises like that, just a few plaintive, pathetic miauws to which nobody could possibly object. At first Mrs White had decided to bear it patiently, on the assumption that it could not last very long. Mrs Knox, next door, must be having the baby for a visit, she supposed, for it was obviously not her own. She decided to wait it out with Christian resignation.

Her policy seemed to have paid off, when the noises ceased after a fortnight and nappies could no longer be seen fluttering on the other side of the hedge. So imagine the horror when a week later it started up again, babies whining night and day; it was such a penetrating noise, Mrs White complained, it went through and through her head. It made one understand how those baby-batterers ticked; sometimes her hands positively itched to smack the infant when it had been crying non-stop for hours. There must be something wrong with the child; no healthy, well-trained baby was so remorselessly awake.

So after bearing the disturbance with, she thought, commendable patience, Mrs White went round to call.

Mrs Knox opened the door after a considerable delay, swathed in a towelling apron, looking flushed and dishevelled. No middle-aged woman, Mrs White thought, should let herself be seen like that.

She had been prepared to probe tactfully, and discover how long the child would be staying. Putting a date to the end of the torment might lessen it. Mrs White described the encounter to her assistant, still flushed with fury.

'Can you conceive of it, Jill, will you believe me when I tell you that the woman is actually giving these children a foster home? She will be having them indefinitely, one after another, always new-born, crying and wailing like buzz saws. I shall go demented, quite demented. Aren't you sorry for me?'

Jill's shining hair swung forward over her face as she nodded, but she went on filing her nails, and she had not, in fact, heard more than one word in three. Her employer bored her almost at much as the antiques they sold.

'I shall see my solicitor, I'm sure it is an actionable nuisance. And what about planning permission? Don't you need a licence to be a foster parent? I shall object. She should be inhibited,' Mrs White declared, echoing Mrs Proudie. She felt that insult had been added to injury by her neighbour's brazen lack of concern. Mrs Knox had evidently felt that she deserved congratulations rather than censure for her public-spirited profession. She had displayed a large nursery – facing towards Sylvia White's bedroom – decorated in pastel colours, frills and cartoon transfers, and proudly explained how she ensured that the babies had perfectly balanced diets and unending fresh air. The window, it seemed, was only closed at bath time. She had looked with a maudlin smile at the squalling creature in the cradle.

'This cross chap is called John,' she said. 'I always call the boys John and the girls Mary. It lets me forget that I shall have to give them back.' She hitched the baby competently on to her shoulder and it gulped at once, sobbed and fell asleep. 'There, that's all he needed.' She led the way downstairs for coffee, pointing to the pram waiting under the tree nearest to Mrs White's garden and explaining how the nappies were always triple-rinsed and aired. 'So lucky that there aren't any restrictive covenants about hanging out washing,' she said, laughing, 'there easily might have been in a district like this. But Alan was determined to move here, it's always been his ambition.'

Sylvia White was having difficulty in hiding her mounting fury at the assumption that she should not only tolerate but also admire and be interested in the brats. It was unbearable not to be able to lose her temper now, but something told her that stealth would be the best strategy. One could always tell with this sort of square-set middle-aged woman that opposition would strengthen her resolve. So she murmured politenesses with great self-control, and sipped the weak coffee; it was, as a matter of fact, almost soothing to collect up with her eye the full catalogue of horrors which Mrs Knox chose to furnish her house – mock-antiques and ill-designed modern stuff side by side. There was a picture of a Eurasian girl with greenish skin, and a small tapestry picture in a large frame hung very high on the wall.

She said with a sweet smile: 'Doesn't your husband object to the babies – dear little things?'

'He's really never here to notice them. He's always away during the week – foreign sales manager, in Ladies' Outerwear, you know – and if he's been abroad he doesn't always come home at the weekends. He's glad to think I have the company. I did it for years in our old home – but it's taken me a little while to get straight here. I'm ever so glad to have the babies again now.'

Sylvia White had tried to convey some of the anguish she felt when her ears were assailed by infantile wailing but it did not seem to register upon Mrs Knox, and though taking a polite leave she went on to the shop fuming.

It was typical of the way life treated poor widows like herself, she realized, when her solicitor was of no help whatever and refused to concern himself with suing for nuisance. He said that the crying of one or two small babies in a properly run home, or foster home, was not capable of being a nuisance in the eyes of the law; he would not be giving her the best of his professional advice if he allowed her to proceed with such an action. The most he reluctantly agreed to do was to find out whether Mrs Knox was licensed with the Orton Corporation as a foster mother. He took ages to find this out; Mrs White had repeatedly to telephone his office before getting anything out of him. He was protected by batteries of underlings, and it seemed almost impossible to get through to him; and it was not as though she didn't pay for his so-called services.

Eventually he informed her that Mrs Knox was properly registered with the childrens' department, having been inspected, evaluated and checked for material comfort and emotional soundness down to the last detail. In fact, the Children's Officer had informed Simpkin, Simpkin and Johns, in an unregulated confidence, Mrs Knox provided the ideal home for foster children and they only wished there were more like it. Young Mr Simpkin indulged himself in what Mrs White regarded as unwarranted facetiousness by suggesting that she might like to start up as a foster mother herself – 'Keep each other company – what?'

So it seemed that there was nothing she could do. It was like a motorway coming at the end of the garden, or being compulsorily purchased for council houses – the innocent householder was always ground under. Mrs White wrote to her son that she was in despair and would probably have to move house again, but she took no steps to do so. It seemed too unfair that she should be driven out of a very comfortable residence in a most desirable district by one selfish, inconsiderate neighbour. And from time to time there were respites, when the noises ceased and she could imagine that they might not, this time, start again, when the only wails one heard in the twenty-four hours were her poor pussies asking for an early dinner. But 'an ideal foster mother' was too valuable to waste, and always, just as Mrs White thought the agony was over, along would come that hateful little van and deliver another mewling, puking infant. By chance, Mrs White happened to be watching several times when the deliveries were made. She grew quite to hate the sight of any grey mini vans, though there were only two which delivered the infants; one was marked with the crest of Orton County Council, and the other had a small sign on the side which read 'Mary and Martha Maternity Homes'. She could not find it in the Orton telephone book, but Mrs Knox had told her, with the same infuriating smugness which characterized all her remarks about her profession, that she had a sort of contract with a maternity home outside the city and she kept herself available for their cases, as well as those sent via the Children's Department.

The driver of the private van was usually the same person, a dark-skinned woman who wore sun glasses and a peaked uniform cap over her thick, long-fringed hair. Mrs White knew it was no good approaching the council, but she had sometimes wondered whether it might be worth appealing to this woman's better nature, and begging her to cease employing Margaret Knox, but it seemed impossible to get hold of her. She would whisk her little car in at the Knoxes' drive, going far too quickly with a baby in the car, and once even nearly running over one of the Persian cats, which was promenading with grace and dignity along the pavement. But the woman drove right in, down beside the garage, where she was screened from view by a woven fence, and she would always stay for a while, presumably putting the infant to bed and discussing its horrid needs, before she left again at great speed.

Sylvia White realized – when she was in a good mood and the day had gone well – that she was not being reasonable about this. But even at good times, the back of her mind was resentful, and on other days the whole subject seemed like a gigantic cloud over everything. She would find herself listening for the cries, bracing herself when they ceased for their inevitable recommencement, even turning off the television so as to make sure that they were still there.

Visitors were unimpressed by her sufferings, and refused to admit that they heard anything. One went so far as to suggests that the mewing of the cats might be more disturbing to a neighbour than the more natural, as she dared to call it, crying of a baby. It was all that Sylvia White could do not to go and wring the child's neck on fine days when it lay broadcasting its presence in the garden to the wide world.

It was all aggravated by the lack of sympathy of everyone she knew. Even her son had written from Salt Lake City telling her that she was making a terrible fuss about nothing. But he always had been an insensitive boy.

This went on for several months; and Sylvia White con-

22

cluded that she would either have to bring the situation to
an end by moving house again, and really she did not see
why she should be driven away by this more than usual lack
of consideration, or by taking steps to end the nuisance
herself. It was obvious that the authorities would not help
even if it were killing her – and it might come to that. A
sensitive person could easily die from such treatment; it was
like the Chinese water torture, a continual torment.

Therefore, Mrs Margaret Knox must be stopped, and
she, Sylvia herself, must see to it.

IV

It had been too dark to see more than the man's bulky
silhouette, but he was placeable by the smell of cigars and
expensive sweat, unnaturally altered from a masculine
acridity by the superimposition of musk-scented lotions.
He was grunting and panting; but then so were all the other
men in the room. Indeed, Sarah thought, she seemed to be
the only person there not merging into the physical.

She heaved herself ungently up, displacing the man, who
fell back sharply on to the thick carpet. He tugged at her
legs as she stood above him, rubbing his hand upwards
along the curve of her thigh, reaching up to fumble in the
damp stubble. In her eagerness for new experience Sarah
had followed the advice of a sex pundit and tried shaving in
unusual places; without, as far as she could tell, making
much difference. Another old wives', or perhaps young
bachelors', tale.

The man, whose name, as far as she could remember,
was Keith, muttered something cross and pulled and poked
as she tried to adjust her dress. She kicked his upper arm
and said:

'Do stop it. Leave me alone.'

'Oh, come on, darling.' His voice was slurred and sod-
den. 'Can't stop in the middle like that.'

23

'Why not?'

'It's not fair. Come on, we'll have some fun.'

'You're so wrong, my fumbling friend.' She stepped over him and tore her ankle from his grasp as he shouted after her:

'Prick-teasing bitch.'

None of the other couples took any notice as she edged around or over them on the way to the stairs. The first three bedrooms she looked into were blatantly occupied, but the baby's room was empty since the cot would hardly have accommodated a pair of midgets and the floor was hard. Sarah went in and shut the door, and sat down on the child's chair. She rubbed some baby lotion absent-mindedly into her hands. The Firths' children's grandparents probably had them to stay so often that spares of equipment were kept at their house. One could hardly, after all, have this sort of party if a six-year-old might appear in the middle of it.

It would have been nice to go home, but she felt shy about braving the obstacles between herself and the front door. In any case, any outraged virtue which one might have dared to display twenty years ago must be kept strictly secret. Nowadays one was ashamed not to share in licence.

Sarah smoothed back her hair with her hands, and wished that her bag, containing cigarettes, make-up and car keys, was not also irretrievably in the room downstairs. This nursery provided no diversion but Andy Pandy. She wondered whether she was stuck up here till dawn – what was the technique of escape? The Firths' friends were mostly youngish and not all that rich, which explained why the couples had stayed in the house, though no doubt some of the parked cars had interesting dramas going on in them. At the Waldorfs, last week, everybody had gone off to rich houses in plushy cars, even if the key lottery couldn't ensure plushy men. Sarah and Jeffrey had cheated, and gone home virtuously together; and had then spent the rest of the night waking up to giggle at the thought of whom they might have found themselves beside.

The Fosters were still learning the customs of Orton. It

24

was funny to remember how they had been used, in the olden days, to drive around it on the by-pass, going to Skye, and ask each other who could bear to live somewhere so dreadful? It must have been just about here, three years ago, that she had suddenly discovered that the front seats of their new estate car reclined, and shot herself backwards on to Marcus's car seat, giving herself a nasty crack on the head. It was the first real car they had achieved, after a succession of battered vans, and they had bemoaned the fact that reclining front seats had come their way years too late. Now she wondered whether they were not in fact manu-factured for an older age group. She started to invent advertising slogans for 'Wife-swapping in comfort'. It was nice to be sure that Jeffrey, far from wife-swapping on his reclining seats, was chastely and virtuously lecturing to a seminar on urban housing schemes.

With tactful quiet the door opened a little, but when Margaret Knox saw that there was only one women, de-cently disposed on a chair, she came right into the room and propped herself on the radiator.

'You escaping too?'

Sarah nodded, and avidly accepted a cigarette. She and Margaret Knox had met at a coffee morning earlier in the summer, and it was a surprise to see her here this evening, uncompromisingly respectable in appearance, in a dark blue dress with waved and bouffant hair. All the other women had mounds of curls and ringlets, and dresses either tightly provocative or deeply revealing, and Sarah herself had made some effort over her appearance, though there was not much you could do with long straight hair and a fringe but put heavy make-up on the eyes beneath the undergrowth.

'Actually, I've been in the kitchen,' Mrs Knox said. 'There's a terrific display of goodies for later, which I've made some inroads on. Mounds of smoked salmon.'

'Oh. I am hungry, as a matter of fact. But I don't want to run into – Keith, I think his name is.'

'Did you stand him up?'

'Well – he was standing up.' Mrs Knox giggled, and Sarah asked her: 'Are parties in Orton always like this?'

'Oh no, I shouldn't think so. Sometimes just a bit of kissing and cuddling, and the odd light left on. I think the Firths are trying to keep up with the Joneses, or outdo them. That's why I went off to the food, it's all a bit much for me. Not that my husband seems to mind it.'

'Don't you care if he's – well, joining in?'

'Wouldn't make much difference if I did.' Mrs Knox sounded momentarily bitter, but quickly cheered up, and said, 'I suppose you haven't lived around here very long?'

'No. We moved in March. We've got a house in East Trenton.'

'A very select district, my dear. We live near here. This is the only other part of Orton people like us live in – the young executives' dream.'

'Are those – baboons – downstairs all young executives then? No wonder I can't bear them. I never met anyone in business in my life before we moved here.'

'Oh no, once they arrive here they're the bosses. The Waldorfs, for example: he's the young master at Makepiece's, his grandfather started the firm. Gerry Firth, downstairs, he's just taken over the family concern, kitchen gadgets. What is your husband, if he's not in business?'

'He's an architect. He's come to work in the city architect's department. He was in private practice before, until we realized he was too unworldly to make a go of it. But all our friends were architects and painters, that's why it seems so strange here.'

'I can see that it must. Look, come along, I'll give you a lift and you can pick up your car keys tomorrow.'

'Thanks awfully – I would like to go.'

The two women walked through the gloom of the upstairs passage. There was not much sound from the big room downstairs, apart from isolated giggles and squeals and a rather sinister drum beat from the record player. They stepped cautiously down the stairs, past three embraced couples, towards the warm, stirring darkness below. It reminded Sarah unpleasantly of a stable at night, with the hot, snuffling animals shifting about on the straw, ready to distribute sleepy kicks. This likeness was intensified when a damp hand seized her by the upper arm and a voice said loudly,

'Here she is, the teasing bint. Come on, lovely, it isn't fair to keep me waiting like that.' A few of the dark mounds moved and a head appeared above the back of the sofa. In the firelight Marion Firth could be seen dishevelled, but still dressed, long curls from her towering hair fallen over her face. She called, 'Anything wrong?' and giggled, and then a languid hand on her head pulled her back to its owner's embrace.

Sarah achieved the front door with relief, pleased by the wet tarmac and peace outside. In the dark, the suburb seemed agreeably rural, but by daylight there were few signs visible of the farm the land had been less than three-quarters of a century before. It was traceable now only in the names of the houses, like Elmfield, Barncroft and Longacre.

Margaret Knox conducted Sarah by torchlight through various vestigial field paths, now dark alleys, towards her house. Sarah lost her sense of direction almost at once and followed blindly, stumbling along in her silly shoes.

'Why did you go to a party like that?' said Mrs Knox, but not in a censorious voice.

'Oh, I'm so bored I'll go to anything. What on earth is there to do in Orton? It's like living in a desert, after London.'

Mrs Knox turned into a gravel drive, and fumbled for her key at the garage door. A faint sound of baby crying came from near by and Sarah said,

'Yours are tiny, are they?' in a tone which implied complicity and experience – a 'we're all in it together' voice.

'No, I'm a foster mother,' the other woman answered briefly.

'How noble of you,' Sarah said sincerely. 'My own babies were more than enough for me.'

'Well, I haven't any of my own. I don't often have these ones at the weekend, in fact, my husband doesn't like it. I had two this week and this one got left too long. I usually manage to get them taken back before he comes home – he's away on business during the week. It meant getting a schoolgirl in to baby-sit.'

Mrs Knox backed out of the garage, and drove Sarah home with impressive adherence to the Highway Code. She didn't talk but concentrated on driving, though she seemed pleased to come into Sarah's house for some coffee, after kindly driving home Sarah's baby-sitter.

The two women sat at the dining table with their steaming mugs. Sarah was relaxed, having unbuttoned her tight dress and taken off her shoes. Mrs Knox sat rather primly as though at Sunday lunch, and held the heavy china as though it were a porcelain demi-tasse. She had a heavy, sallow skinned face, and though she spoke unaccented English retained traces of regionalism; she said ninet-een, and rhymed 'one' with 'don'. Her enquiries seemed more polite than interested, and Sarah made her usual rehearsed replies to them; they were settling in well in Orton, she said, and expected to be very happy there; the children attended the local primary school, which was run by the most enlightened education authority in the country – no, they couldn't actually read very well yet, but they had such fun, and the other children were so nice.

'And you've made some friends, have you?'

'Well, we haven't met very many people yet. I'm sure we shall, though. The parents fetching from school all look very nice.' In fact, Sarah thought, but did not say, the parents all looked clean and middle-class. In a town which had one of the highest proportions of immigrants, there did not seem to be one Negro or Indian child at this primary school; typical, Sarah smugly felt, of what she disliked in Orton. And all the women she had met had been immersed in a life which she had thought only existed in the imaginations of advertising copy-writers. Everybody seemed to exude prosperity and complacency. Everything in Orton was for the best in the best of all possible worlds, and no disturbing influence would be allowed to check the march of progressive primary schools, supermarkets, roads and golf clubs. Sarah realized that she must conform to the rule

28

of two or three children, two or three motor-cars, member-
ship of two or three sports clubs, yearly holidays in the
anglicized parts of the Mediterranean, monthly trips to
London for a matinee, weekly trips to hairdresser and
supermarket, or remain for ever alien.

The awful, insidious thing, Sarah thought, as she shut the
front door after Margaret Knox, was that it would be so
easy to be submerged in this life. It was all arranged for
comfort and convenience. These women would have had
mothers whose days were filled with the hard domestic
labour which their own batteries of machines made unnecessary; or, if their mothers had been employers of servants, they would have watched them doing work which the
welfare state had now taken over. They did not want to go
back to work as secretaries or physiotherapists, and fortunately the demands of school holidays and husbands whose
working day finished at five gave a complete excuse not to
do that. So the day had to be filled otherwise; and what
with luncheon clubs and tennis, taking the children swimming and the odd bazaar, so it was.

If only, Sarah thought, for the fiftieth time, she could see
some alternative to this fate for herself. But her own career
had been nonexistent. She had married Jeffrey straight
from art school, where she had not quite finished a course in
metal work. She could not even amuse herself now by
painting anything but the most pathetic daubs.

The fact was, and she realized it, that she was fighting
against being a provincial lady, which was what she was,
what all these other women were, and what she might as
well resign herself to being for the rest of her life. In
London she might go to operas and shop at Habitat and
Harrod's; she would mitigate the tedium and the pinpricks
of married life with children by sharing them with a friend
who displayed the same mixture of rueful resignation and
furious resentment. They would have spoken the same
language. And Jeffrey, too, would have shared his interest
and jokes and his perpetual pots of tea with the same
friend's husband. They would all have been in it together.
But here – the hours, days and years stretched bleakly and

boringly ahead. It was not only from tiredness that Sarah yawned as she climbed laboriously up to bed. 'I wish,' she said aloud, not meaning it, 'I wish that I were dead.'

In the morning, Sarah hardly had time to wish for death, for that required a certain concentration of bitterness. When her emotions were dissipated by irritation with her children, and self-defeating viciousness aimed at them, the most she had time to pine for was to be somewhere else; and with the nasty memory of the fumbling fingers of the stocking manufacturer with whom she had been paired off the evening before fresh in her mind, she realized that it had not been the fact that he wasn't Jeffrey that had disgusted her.

Jeffrey, she felt vaguely, as she devoted what was awake of her intellect to the whereabouts of football boots, Jeffrey loved her and she loved him. He was affectionate, patient, reliable and faithful. And by him, she was bored, bored, bored. He would be a tower of strength in any emergency, her support in times of trouble. But her greatest troubles were what other women prayed to have the opportunity for – the need to decide what to have for lunch, a washing-machine on the blink. The strength which supported could also crush, by its insensibility to minuscule burdens. Jeffrey's virtues were wasted on a woman whose complaints deserved only to be expressed as witticisms.

Not of course, she thought, her intellect waking momentarily from its dream, that she wished for the sort of trouble that one needed a man like Jeffrey to cope with. But at the moment he just couldn't see the point of her moans, and he switched them off in his mind. Which was unfair, when all she wanted was a bit of fun.

V

Sarah got her bit of fun the very next day through the unlikely medium of Margaret Knox; for it was because of her that Sarah renewed acquaintance with Victor Nightingale.

He was a tall, very thin man with flax-pale hair growing thin on top, but still able to call himself young; that at any rate was how he was described in gossip columns. He was a socialist socialite, a handsome man, with thin, smooth skin stretched tight over elegant bones; his head proved, Sarah thought, that skulls were the result of a dead head, which was the sort of thing a protected person like herself tended to believe because she was told so, not because of personal knowledge. With so many people, the logic of anatomy was hidden by the folds and curves of its covering. Victor had a childish, angled profile and advertisement-standard teeth. He had a trick of jerking his china-blue gaze back to whomever he was speaking to, as though his agent had insisted that people he was canvassing must feel they had his full attention. Sarah had always doubted that eyes could hold expressions; but his did look sincere and compelling. Sarah thought he was marvellous. To her, he positively smelt of the big wide world she craved.

Not that it was a very smart place to meet him in. Sarah was on her way to London for the day. The motorway was wet and greasy and after two hours of competitive driving, hands clenched on the wheel and feet rigidly poised above the pedals, she had felt her arms beginning to shake and that ominous heaviness of the eyelids which concentration induces. She had pulled in to the motorway cafe, hating the look of it and the juke-box audible above the traffic's roar, and had gone into the self-service to buy a cup of tea and a moist cheese sandwich. It had been a considerable surprise to see Mrs Knox at one of the narrow tables; her trim, tight form, the waves of the hair, seemed out of place in this noisy haven of the common man. One did not visualize Margaret Knox loading a tin tray with cafeteria food.

Vic Nightingale must have chosen the cafeteria instead of the waitress service because he was less likely to be recognized there. He was not a television politician, but tended to aim his publicity at highbrows. He wrote pamphlets about housing conditions and book reviews for the *New Statesman*; his photograph sometimes appeared at the head of a column in *The Times*. He had two cups of black coffee in front of him and was half way through the first one. Margaret Knox, neatly sitting on the other side of the table, was sipping at the cardboard cup, holding the saucer at chest level beneath it. On her plate was a bath bun, which she had cut into small cubes, and popped into her mouth like those little black boys which collect for charities; whenever they went to the grocer Sarah had to give Emily a penny to put into his palm, and watch and exclaim as it jerked the coin upwards into its grinning metal maw.

Sarah slid in beside Margaret, and said, in that clear and carrying voice which Jeffrey said branded her to half the world as an enemy, 'Hullo, Margaret, what fun. Are you having a binge?'

Margaret was just explaining that she was on her way to return the most recent John to the children's home, when Sarah realized at whom she was looking. She leant forward eagerly, ignoring Margaret's disapproving frown.

'It's Victor Nightingale, isn't it? Do you remember, we met a couple of years ago, at the Garrowbys' Hogmanay party in Canonbury Square. I'm Sarah Foster.'

With perfect equanimity and apparent pleasure the young man admitted to recalling the evening, and putting away his papers into a small briefcase on the floor, made formal enquiries about where the Fosters lived now, and what Sarah was doing these days.

'Oh well, we're exiled in the Midlands, too dull to tell about. I'm sorry, Margaret, this is Mr Nightingale. Mrs Knox. Anyway, I'm going to London for a bit of escape. I'm like that Greek giant who derived his strength from mother earth and was mightier every time he fell on it – I have to charge myself up in London sometimes.'

Conversation could not be fluent in such surroundings, and Margaret Knox's slightly basilisk eye inhibited the arch banter with which Sarah often made conversation to strange men; experience had proved its efficacy, particularly with men older than herself. Vic Nightingale was agreeable and polite, not more, but Sarah would have overlooked positive rudeness. She drove off having got herself invited to drinks at Vic's house that evening, and hummed down the motorway very cheerfully. Even her car seemed in better form.

Without compunction Sarah cancelled her dentist's appointment, and made straight for the West End; she passed a happy day enduring the battering of a masseuse, the patronizing of a glamorous chit in a beauty salon and the flattery of a saleswoman. Thus armoured, Sarah had sufficient self-confidence to get her as far as Sloane Square. But she went up the King's Road with increasing nervousness. It was years since she had experienced this purely social fright, a chilly apprehension prickling on the back of her neck, a fermenting of the lower digestive tract. She hoped it was more than the eye of faith and hope which had made her pleased with her appearance. The trouble was, she had to admit, that scorn the provincialism of Orton as she would, once she trod the streets of London she stopped feeling at all metropolitan. Perhaps, she thought in a panic, perhaps I've blended in already. Perhaps Vic will introduce me as a little friend up from the Midlands for the day.

It was a dry, cool evening, and in other circumstances it would have been a treat for Sarah to stroll beside the bizarre and seductive Chelsea shops, unhurried and unbadgered. She had arrived too early and purposely parked her car some distance from Vic's address. Now her steps grew slower and her mirrored image no longer pleased. But when she was already twenty minutes after the time appointed, she felt obliged to turn down towards the river, and along the street of tarted-up workmen's cottages to Vic Nightingale's house. It was spick with white paint and brass door furniture. Through the barred basement window was a large kitchen where a manservant's back was visible taking ice from a catering-sized refrigerator. The curtains were drawn across the ground-floor windows and Sarah could not hear any cocktail-party buzz from inside. Her hand was trembling as she rang the bell, and she took off, and nervously pulled on again, her new kid gloves. Vic opened the front door himself.

There were about half a dozen people in the drawing-room, and Sarah shook hands with them all, hoping that the nervous twitch of her lips could be felt but not seen. She accepted a glass of gin, and, calmed by alcohol, was able to converse politely with a young man in a striped tie who appeared to be a banker.

None of the other people there seemed to be either very smart or very young and Sarah was soon able to forget her picture of herself as an elderly dowd. Indeed, her reflection in the gilt glass above the mantelpiece showed her an irreproachably correct young woman with lacquered hair and a self-confident expression. So she tried to live up to her appearance.

Vic Nightingale's drawing-room was curiously conventional. The furniture was new, but in the antique style, piecrust tables and bow-fronted chests with the smooth uncracked gleam which proclaimed that they came from Harrods, not the antique shop down the road. There were a couple of 'drawing-room pictures' – nameless rural oil paintings – and some unremarkable china in the corner cupboard. The upholstery was velvet, the curtains brocade, the whole proclaiming its class and type, as though in uniform. There were no photographs, or open books; only a stack of invitations on the mantelpiece and some magazines laid out on the table in the window as though in a doctor's waiting room. One could only conclude, thought Sarah, that Vic Nightingale's life was geared entirely to an audience, and that he had no private activities or secrets.

It was a dull enough party, after Sarah's anticipatory heart burnings. The only other woman was Felicity Armitage, whom Sarah had in fact recognized from photographs; the right sort of girl for an ambitious politician,

34

related to half the Tory hierarchy and rich as well. If she married a Socialist it would pull votes in for him by the hundred. Everybody called her Folly, and she seemed very much at home.

When a couple of people had left, Sarah thought she had better do so herself rather than stay and be a bore; she had arranged to spend the night at her parents' house in St John's Wood before going back to Orton – Jeffrey was looking after the children – and wondered glumly whether to take herself to the cinema, never very tempting alone, or to drop in on a friend. She was surprised when Folly Armitage came up to say goodbye to her, and to express pleasure at having met her. 'It's such fun meeting Vic's old friends,' she said, and before Sarah could disclaim had whisked out, and her chummy and cheerful goodnights to the man at the door faded into the roar of her sports car. Vic dropped the curtain back over the window – he had been standing waving to her – and the farewell smile switched off his face.

He came to stand beside Sarah, and said in a low voice, 'Will you have dinner with me? We might go out somewhere.' It needed no consideration for Sarah to accept. But as she stood then by the fire – a competently built pile of illegal, smoking logs, in a gleaming steel grate – feeling the totally different sensations of the dinner guest waiting for the tiresome drinkers to depart, instead of wondering how soon she must leave others to dine themselves, she spread her manicured left hand surreptitiously out, as though warming her hands, and looked guiltily at her wedding-ring. Often as she had thought of Jeffrey with anger and annoyance, often as she had wondered whether the only way to relieve the monotony of her life would be to leave him and go back to a flat in London; often, indeed, as she had flirted at London parties, and even with the memory of her experiments at the last Orton party, still, there seemed something infinitely naughtier about actually going out to dinner, in London, with a strange man who did not know, and therefore had no loyalty of friendship to her husband.

In theory Sarah despised the very idea that friendships were impossible between man and woman. She would have dismissed it as unutterably bourgeois and bigoted if anyone else had said to her that she should not dine with a man friend, alone. But the occasion had never arisen before. And she felt a squirm of delightful naughtiness at the prospect.

She watched impatiently as the four remaining men chatted and drank as though settled for the evening. They were the sort of men whom Sarah would have liked to find herself despising. The liberal academic habits of her parents' lives, and the free attitudes of her art school and architecty friends, the people with whom her adult life had been lived, had bred in Sarah prejudices as conventional as those of the plummy-voiced, gilded youths who were now sounding off about the gold standard and iniquitous taxation. A predictable conversation, no doubt duplicated by the dozen in all the other pretty little houses around here; and only different in degree from the lists of fast cars and Spanish holidays which Sarah's Orton neighbours would now be discussing over their cocktails. Yet tonight there seemed something attractive and enviable about these young men. It was immensely reassuring to be in the company of people who never had to doubt themselves.

But as they left, trooping out in a group, calling in self-confident voices, 'Goodnight, Buddle,' Vic said. 'Good chaps. I hope you liked them. Old Williams is a remarkable fellow, you know, father's a Trade Unionist in some coal mine, South Wales or something, won't admit to his friends that David's gone over to the enemy. He's a genius, got a real feel for the market.'

Sarah accepted another drink so as to have something to do with her hands, and said politely, 'How interesting. Do tell me, where is your constituency? So silly of me not to know.'

'Not at all, why should you? Actually it's not far from Orton, Ferraby West. I was down there all yesterday, kissing babies and what not. Had to smooth over the change of policy about the fixed rent scheme. Though it should be a safe enough seat, actually.'

'You lose votes if you change your mind, do you?'

'Oh, well, bound to a bit. But it should be all right so

long as I do what I'm told – follow the party policy and all that.'

'You mean if your bosses change their minds?' Sarah was given to asking outrageous questions as though she really wanted to know the answer. It had been part of her technique when making her way as a girl at parties; she would beg people to tell her what they actually did all day, how many hours a solicitor spent asleep at his desk, or what a colour supplement's resident cartoonist earned.

Now for a moment Vic Nightingale seemed to hesitate about taking offence, but then he laughed lightly and said, 'You have to vote according to the whips, naturally. You make yourself felt behind the scenes if you want to.'

'It seems a bit undemocratic.'

'This country is undemocratic. There's too large a population – mostly morons – for it to be anything else. Things have to get done somehow.'

Sarah popped her eyes at him, and asked, 'Is that what you really think?' and he said hurriedly, 'No, of course I don't, I was joking. Forget I spoke. What about dinner?'

Sarah took her time in the bathroom, which was modishly decorated with a frieze wallpaper of the Bayeux Tapestry – *Haroldus interfectus est* inescapably to the eye as she sat on the lavatory – and old chemists' drug jars. She sneaked a quick look into the cupboard: a large variety of ointments and unguents and an expensive French lipstick.

Dinner was expensive and conversation oiled. Sarah felt no special frisson of attraction for Vic – he was so different from Jeffrey that she supposed he was not her type, and she had to pretend interest in the things he talked about, though by dredging from her memory the reviews and comments from last Sunday's papers she was able to answer. As she drank bedtime tea with her parents, and described their grandchildren's antics, Sarah recognized that the flattery of his attention added to his charm – and he had lots of that. If he liked her, she would certainly take care to like him.

Sarah drove back to Orton with her imagination whirling with pictures of fun in store. She had made a date to meet Victor again quite soon; and the prospect of what would happen that time both excited and horrified her. One could not, nowadays, refuse to sleep with a man simply because one was married to another one, Sarah told herself, and anybody who lived in Vic's world would take it for granted that scruples of that nature were years out of date. Whether one actually wanted to do it was another matter. But presumably payment in kind must be made. With a little smile on her face, Sarah thought of the immediate future. As long as one wasn't provincial and bourgeois about things which everybody accepted were unimportant, there should be some treats to come. After all, one didn't want to sit on one's death-bed having memories of only one man. One needed a standard of comparison. Think what one might be missing.

VI

It seemed much easier to bear the return to real life, with a titillating thought at the back of her mind, and Sarah was unusually patient with Marcus and Emily. But she could never be anything but grumpy at breakfast, her family must just learn to accept it. The next day she got up, sulking as usual at the horror of a world that obliged one to surface at half-past seven.

Marcus had inherited Sarah's matutinal malaise and getting him off to school was an obstacle race of remarks which might hurt his feelings and reduce him to time-wasting tears, or worse, to a determination not to go to school at all. His 'tummy was sore' at the slightest provocation.

When the door bell rang it was like the moment of denouement in a radio play, all screams and crossness momentarily suspended. Jeffrey allowed a stubborn look to overcome his face before burying it in the paper again, so Sarah was obliged to go herself, trailing gingerly down the slippery wooden stairs in her long dressing-gown.

The man who waited there was extremely tall, and thin,

bending forwards like the poplars which marked off the little estate. He had a disproportionately small head and a pointed chin superimposed on a discreet little double chin, and he looked mild and shy. He sighed when he was confronted by an unwelcoming crack in the front door, and Sarah opened it wider to stand revealed in grubby nylon quilting.

'I say, I'm awfully sorry, Mrs Foster.' His voice was tenor and pleasant, and Sarah realised who he was. She said, more cordially than he expected,

'You must be Mr Millington, from next door, are you? Do come in.' She immediately repented of this rash invitation, but he stayed hovering on the doorstep, and Sarah turned to yell, 'Get ready, children, will you? Clean your teeth and go to the lavatory. Sorry.' She turned back to the man, who was now blushing under smoothly shaved, grey skin.

'You see, it sounds so awful, but I thought perhaps – another woman, you know ...' He was looking at her hopefully, but Sarah looked mystified and he was forced to go on,

'It's Flora. That's my wife.'

'What about her, Mr Millington?'

'Well, you see, she only came back yesterday, she's been with her mother. In Surrey. I expect you were wondering why you hadn't seen her.'

'Well, no, not actually.'

'Oh well, anyway,' he said hurriedly, brushing that aside, 'the thing is that I don't like to leave her. Alone here. All day, d'you see, while I'm out.'

'Why not?' It was too early in the morning for Sarah to be tactful.

'The thing is, you see,' he leant forward over Sarah with an access of self-confidence, 'it's since the baby was born. Cherry. She's one month old.' His oddly expressive, plaintive face broke into a proud smile, and then he quickly recovered gravity. 'She's depressed after the baby. And being lonely here. We're new to Orton. And I don't like to leave her. So I thought ...' He spread his hands out in a helpless gesture, and Sarah, who was prepared to be hostile, since nothing annoyed her more than the prospect of sick-visiting, was disarmed.

'You want me to go in and see her, is that it?'

'What it is, you see, the fact is that she's shy. She won't come to you, not when you are strangers. She'd be ever so cross if she thought I'd asked you.' He glanced up at the windows of his own house, and backed slowly away down the path. 'So I thought – it's so kind of you – thank you very much – good morning.' Raising his grey trilby to reveal a pointed, thin-haired skull, he frankly fled, without a backward glance, into his own garage.

Sarah turned to meet her own family coming down the stairs. It was Jeffrey's turn to deliver the children to school – a chore he reluctantly undertook, and daily at fetching time Sarah dropped hints to the other mothers about rotas, so far unproductively. Sarah told him as he passed what her neighbour had wanted. Jeffrey apparently paid no attention, gripped by morning abstraction, but Sarah always worked her bad temper off on him. 'The very idea,' she complained, 'saying I should go just because I'm another woman. Half the human race, after all – And I don't feel much sympathy for anyone who's scared to be alone, I must say.'

Jeffrey revved out of the garage and the car hiccupped off to the battlefield which the roads of rush-hour Orton constituted. Sarah returned to her coffee and the *Guardian*; she would have a bath and do the weekly supermarket trip. If there was time she might call next door, though it was a bit much to expect. But she found herself putting on a new matching skirt and jersey, and unladdered tights. Her subconscious had clearly decided to take her calling on Flora Millington today.

The house next door was identical on the exterior with the Fosters' own, but for a yellow front door instead of an olive-green one. There were nappies in the garden – and complaints in store from the Haywoods, no doubt, who had already objected to Sarah's outside clothesline – but no baby in a pram although the day was fine, and Sarah supposed that Flora Millington had gone out. She was already on her way back home when the front door bell was answered, and only turned when a throat was cleared, and a timid voice enquired, 'I'm so sorry – did you ring?'

Flora Millington was at least twenty years younger than her husband; that was the first thought to spring to mind at the sight of her, quickly followed by the realization that she looked like an ally. Sarah was cheerful as she followed her up to the living-room. She had already forgotten the husbandly hints which had led her to call in the first place.

A woman in Health Visitor's uniform was on the sofa, cradling a baby, and continuing the sentence which had been begun before the interruption.

'But you should leave her outside, Mrs Millington, dear little thing, that will put the roses in her cheeks. You are so lucky to have space for the pram, just what the poppet needs. Now, you show me her warm things, dear, and I'll just pop her down in the garden for her nap, shall I? and then you can have a nice sit-down with a nice cup of coffee.'

Flora Millington picked the baby gently from the plump woman's arms and rocked her to and fro. The child was pale, but looked healthy enough. 'I think I'll just put her in her cradle,' she murmured.

'Now, dear, you must remember what I said. I'm trained to this, you know, that's what I'm here for, to advise you how to take care of your children. Your taxes pay for me, did you know that? You mustn't think that I'm interfering, but do take my advice. Children need good fresh air the same as they need food and sleep. And it's not as though you lived in a horrid dark alley full of traffic. The ideal surroundings for babies, here.'

Flora Millington looked helplessly at the Health Visitor, and said, 'I'll put her beside the open window.'

Sarah interrupted, using her most arrogant voice.

'Don't worry about her now, Nurse,' she said. The Health Visitor looked up in surprise having hardly noticed there was somebody else in the room in her purposeful concentration. 'I've just come to help Mrs Millington. I'll show you out, shall I?' With a firm hand she conducted the Health Visitor downstairs and said a haughty goodbye. It really was a bit much when they came and bullied people like this, she thought – that really *was* a waste of rates and taxes.

'What was all that about?' she asked, going up to the living-room again.

Flora was wiping her eyes, and hastily shoved the handkerchief into her sleeve. She answered; 'Oh, it's all so silly. I – I just can't take being got at like that, though. It makes me feel so helpless. Just – well, Cherry's got a bit of a cold, and I thought I'd keep her in. It's much colder here than in the south anyway.'

'Well, that's all right. Why was she making all that fuss? You put the baby upstairs if you want to.'

It turned out that the Millingtons had lived in Orton for nearly a year, but that Flora had been back at home with her mother for most of the time, sitting on a sofa with high blood pressure at first, and then staying at home after Cherry was born because she felt so helpless with a baby. She had been a student until she was married, and was still vaguely working at her thesis subject – something to do with early Romance languages. The bookcases were full of intimidating dictionaries. Mr Millington was a librarian, and he and Flora had met when he was helping her track down obscure articles through the inter-library loan system.

Once the threat of the Health Visitor was lifted Flora became rather talkative, and produced real coffee and homemade biscuits as though she had expected visitors. She displayed an impressive resignation to Orton, although she had no friends there and was unable to make much progress with her own work as there was no university nearer than Ferraby and consequently no means of checking her references in a large library. She was determined to make the best of it, and said that if one persevered there were one or two pretty corners still to be found, though admittedly most of the town was less attractive than many others.

'It's perfectly hideous,' Sarah said roundly. 'I can't bear the place.'

'I'm not so definite about it. After all, I have to live here, and Cherry will grow up thinking it's home. There's a good convent near here for her, I'm glad to say.'

That explains it, Sarah thought. She had often observed that acceptance of a disagreeable lot came easier to Catholics. She looked around for further data, but the room was non-committally furnished, except for the revealing book-shelves, with a couple of acceptable Renoir reproductions and Victorian furniture. It looked much smaller than Sarah's sitting-room; but then she of course had filled the same space with nothing but a leather chesterfield, a coffee-table and a bentwood rocking-chair.

Chat had continued pleasantly for half an hour when Sarah got up, and was astonished to see an expression of more than social dismay come over Flora's face. She explained: 'It was so nice to have someone to talk to. I – was feeling a little bit lonely. But thank you awfully for coming. Do, please do, come again soon.'

These protestations, continued in a rather high, nervous voice, continued as far as the front door, and Sarah found herself pressing Flora to come to coffee with her the next day. She had not intended to do as much for Mr Millington's appeals, but the right social noises tripped automatically off the tongue; and one could hardly not extend an invitation to somebody who was so plainly begging for it.

VII

Sarah censoriously concluded from her data that all entertaining in Orton took the form of coffee parties for the women and their girl-friends, or of the kind of party which Sarah had experimented with at the Firths' house. She had been to several coffee mornings which were one of Orton's new experiences for her; half a dozen smartly dressed women eating fattening food in a formal room;

most of the women left before twelve to fetch playgroup children home for lunch, but in the one and a half hours, platesful would disappear.

In her reluctance to conform Sarah had so far returned no hospitality of this kind. Margaret Knox had dropped in one morning and been entertained in squalor while Sarah chipped hardened clay from the floor; she had had a brief period of deciding to take up pottery. And Sarah had several times been invited to meet Margaret Knox for coffee, never at her house but in ladylike establishments, where the coffee came in pots and the cakes were home-made.

The two women had little in common, but Margaret seemed to want to keep in touch with Sarah, and her own unrevealing, uncritical way of listening gave a boost to Sarah's ego. It was like having one's private psychiatrist, waiting to note down complaints of boredom, of inability to earn, to work, to be amused. Mrs Knox would sit sipping her drink, nodding and prodding with tactful questions. She seemed interested in everything, and Sarah had even let out her new preoccupation about Vic. Nor did she want the usual payment of women who listen to another's moans: the opportunity to make her own. She said little about her own life, except for explaining that her husband was away so much that she had learnt to live a self-sufficient life.

However, a more intimate relationship was developing slowly. Shortly before Flora's arrival Margaret Knox had been to coffee with Sarah, by arrangement, so that there was a tray ready at least, if not a home-made biscuit to put on it. She sat rocking gently on Sarah's bentwood chair, her head bent over the small bundle in her lap. This was one in a series of babies called Mary, though the first for ages, Margaret said, which was from the private nursing home for whom she did fostering. The council work was almost fully occupying her time now. This was a not un-endearing child, with a great curl of fair hair on the top of her head and wide-awake eyes. She had a small birthmark on her thigh from which Sarah averted her eyes, but she overcame her revulsion from alien flesh long

44

enough to hold the child and to mop up its sour sickness without the held breath and cringing fingertips with which she usually performed this service for other peoples' children. The flesh of her own babies, Sarah had worshipped, and stroked and sniffed at it with sensuous delight, but about others she felt as she did about animals, or about the idea of nursing another adult: it was repellent.

Margaret looked a little blank when Sarah confessed to this defect in herself. 'I don't feel that at all,' she said. 'Specially not with babies, so soft and warm. I love having them to look after. Actually, Mary here really means a lot to me; more than the others.'

'Oh, why? Do you know whose child she is?'

'No, oh no, not that at all. But she's sweet. And then you know, it's quite profitable having her!'

'Really? I thought it was like vocational jobs always are, paid with peanuts.'

'No, well, the council's not very generous, it's true, but the private babies are worth quite a bit more. Aren't you, my duck?'

She rocked calmly, an almost Madonna-like vacancy on her face, and Sarah looked uneasily at her, from behind her mug of coffee. One let out these secrets, blurted things out, she thought, and then regretted it so. Why on earth had she been fool enough to tell Margaret Knox all about Victor? Just because she sat there empty, waiting to be filled with confidences?

Sarah said suddenly, 'Apart from the babies, what do you feel strongly about, Margaret? Oh, I know that sounds silly, but you know so much about me by now!'

The other woman looked up, and for a moment seemed to exude a force of character and concentration which made her unlike any other woman Sarah knew. She said vigorously, 'I'm very interested in politics. I feel most strongly about them.'

'Really?' Sarah knew nothing about politics and could hardly have told which party was in power. Even with Vic, his profession did not impinge on their relationship.

'Yes, I'd give anything to have the power to sort out the

mess we're in. Get rid of the bumbling fools who seem to be trying to ruin us. We need a man like Churchill, only not a Tory, of course, and younger, a real leader again.' Sarah could not remember much about Churchill except that she had seen him in films about the war. But of course Margaret would have been old enough to have done something in the war, to have got the bug of hero worship, which fitted her into a neat pigeonhole.

Sarah asked vaguely, 'Why?'

Margaret's heavy face was brooding and dark above the pale bundle in her arms. Her lower lip jutted like her hero's. 'I suppose I started to feel like this quite a long time ago, as a matter of fact. I had an elder sister, you know, who was massacred by the terrorists in Cyprus. Her husband was in the Forces. And the whole affair was so bungled, our government was so weak, she needn't have died if there had been proper control. And now when we see that man, that clerical devil, lording it over everybody, shaking hands with the Queen, why, he's nothing but a murderer. It makes me realize that our whole system's rotten when things like that can happen.'

Sarah could not answer because she knew nothing about the subject, and because such heat of emotion made her positively uncomfortable; one wasn't used to it. She sat in respectful silence, and then to change the subject said, 'And did you always love babies so much?'

'Yes, I always have. I couldn't have any of my own, which was a terrible disappointment, but perhaps just as well. I had a little cousin, a boy who was a baby when I was nearly grown up, I adored him. Still do, I'd do anything for him. He's turned out to be a wonderful man. But I want to know more about your last trip to London, Sarah,' – for Mrs Knox had come to look after Marcus and Emily the last time that their mother 'had to go up to the dentist' – 'how did it go?'

So Sarah told her far more than she intended to about Vic and his exciting way of life; one had to return confidence for confidence.

The day she met Flora Millington Sarah thought with

some embarrassment of the various revelations she had made to Mrs Knox. She ought to be invited with Flora, but could one rely on her to be more discreet than Sarah had been herself? Sarah looked again at the list she had scribbled on the telephone pad. It had reached a length that made it impossible to delay returning hospitality much longer. If Flora was coming anyway, and Margaret had said she would drop in that day too, it would be a good opportunity to start on it. And she should, she really must try to accept the life in Orton a little more graciously. When she was in a good mood, Sarah knew this perfectly well. And today her self-recriminations were reinforced by a letter in the lunch-time mail from her best friend, who had lived near by in Islington.

'Now, do try to be cheerful about Orton, darling,' Anna wrote, her script sprawling across the page. She did have rather a tendency to dish out good advice, and it was only because she did so with a frank and ingenuous charm that her friends could bear it. 'You may look back on London now as being busy and blissful, but when you were here you spent your time sitting around and moaning that Jeffrey never had time to take you to the theatre or that you hadn't been to a party for six months. So it shouldn't make all that difference even if you do live in a cultural desert. And I'll always be glad to have you to stay if you want a brief fling – you couldn't very well stay with your parents for that. Kisses and hugs to the family, see you soon I hope, much love, A.'

Sarah was not much in the habit of consecutive thought; a fact which had distressed her school teachers and her academic papa, but while she peeled potatoes to make Jeffrey a proper dinner for a change, she reflected intermittently on Anna's remarks. Come to think of it, it was quite true that she and Jeffrey had not gone out very often in London, it was just nice to know that somewhere near by real life was going on. In her temporary moment of self-inspection, Sarah realized that all her life she had glorified the past, resented the present and been pessimistic about the future. Now she lived in Orton she pined for London, but there she had merely kicked against the pricks of early married life and comparative poverty, remembering with nostalgia the freedom of her student days. Yet when she was a student, far from throwing herself with happy abandon into the free life of an art college she had feared to participate, or been shy of the people she would have liked to do things with. And earlier when her family moved into London she had pined for the 'country' in Epsom, moaning about her severance from those suburban horses whose neighing from the Orton potting-sheds now amused her.

The postman had also brought a circular about a Grand Summer Fete at Grande Hall, complete with Funfair, Jumble and Antique Stalls and attractions for all the family, and in her slightly more benevolent mood, Sarah put it on the window-sill. It might be quite fun for the kids, especially since the notice proclaimed that the county schools would have an extra holiday on that date.

Sarah perched on the kitchen stool and sipped instant coffee, and glanced half-heartedly at the paper. She would have to get up a lot of steam before she could force herself to telephone those whom she owed invitations, though she really might as well, since Mrs Knox was due anyway, and it would be good for Flora.

The headlines were still full of the missing Jones baby. There were more photographs of the weeping mother and the pop singer papa being mobbed by sympathetic fans. Pretty Valerie Jones, 21, had been determined to live like other people and not let the money make any difference to her family's life, but now she knew better, Sarah read. When they got the baby back, there'd be no more semi-detached houses, supermarkets and baby clinics for them. They would move to a house in the country, protected by high walls and guard dogs, and have Karen attended by a Harley Street paediatrician. Sarah was shocked to find herself unmoved by a story which she realised should have evoked any mother's sympathy. Babies were, now Emily was six, no longer of personal interest to her, she thought as she went to the telephone.

Flora arrived early, exclaiming about the difference between the two architecturally identical houses. They were in a development of five houses on the site of an Edwardian merchant's palace, tastefully dotted between old trees and chain-link fences. Jeffrey knew that he would have done better himself, but he could just bear the idiom in which they were built. Sarah felt, and told Flora so, that they were a poor exchange for a Victorian terrace house in N.1. The houses were inconveniently on three floors, with an open slatted staircase running through the living area on the middle floor. Even Islington had not accustomed Sarah to the amount of stair-climbing involved when the traditional arrangement of floors was muddled, with Marcus sleeping on the ground floor, his parents and sister on the top, and the kitchen in between. However, as she might have expected, Flora thought it was all marvellous, hers being the first real house she had owned, and Sarah felt inhibited from remarks which would have dimmed that starry-eyed satisfaction.

'I feel quite missionary about your baby,' said Sarah, looking at the tight-tucked carrycot. 'It doesn't look as though she has a cold to me. Why not let's put her outside?'

'Oh, I think I'll just put her upstairs. You don't mind, do you?' Flora looked so anxious that Sarah disclaimed at once. They sat down in the unnaturally tidy room, and Flora picked up, and then politely put down without opening, one of Sarah's pile of colour supplements and trendy glossies.

'You are lucky, I love reading about that sort of world,' Flora said. 'Paris, and New York, and social problems. George doesn't like me to buy them, he says they're degraded.'

'Really? That needn't stop you, I should have thought. They make me feel at home – remind me of how we used to live.'

'Goodness, they feel quite strange to me. I had some in hospital, though. The nurses thought they would take my mind off things.'

'What was wrong with you? Was it just high blood pressure?'

'Well, I got terribly depressed, I'm afraid. They wanted to keep an eye on me. It was better than a mental hospital would have been and I was in rather a state. But it's all fine now, so long as I keep calm and all that. They said I mustn't get too excited. Cherry keeps me well, she's my blessing.'

Sarah was glad to hear the door bell at that point. Almost as much as she hated the idea of looking after another sick person, she hated to hear them talk about their ailments, and it looked as though Flora was just about to launch into an account of 'My Labour'.

Two of the women who had previously invited Sarah to their houses were standing on the doorstep, chattering about a topic of common interest. It turned out that they saw one another continually day and evening, since their husbands were Fraternity brothers. This was one of the customs of Orton before which Sarah's investigations had quite given up, and she had not discovered how it worked. It seemed to be a charitable organization, not a Fraternity in the American sense, and men joined it in order to get on in the local business world; a localized, miniature Rotary Club, perhaps. All the wives spent as much time together as their husbands did, shared holiday villas and baby-sitting, and general togetherness. Sarah had received, in the honeymoon stage of living in Orton, an invitation to persuade Jeffrey to join; her only half joking answer, that she had enough sisters-in-law already, was ill received.

Even Margaret Knox's husband, it turned out when she arrived, was a member of one of these fraternities, but a brief awkwardness seemed to touch the conversation when his name was mentioned, and Mrs Richardson, to change the subject, picked up the local paper from the coffee table and said, 'Did you see, an awful kidnapping again? I've been quite frightened to let Malcolm go to school, I take him to the very door.'

'But it was a new-born baby, wasn't it?' said Sarah, looking at the photograph. It was a blurred family snap showing a tiny child with a coxcomb of hair and two plastic ducks on a rug. The description said she weighed eleven

50

pounds and had a blue mark at the top of the right leg. Sarah would never have thought that the kidnapping of a pop-singer's baby in South London presaged danger to her own school children in the Midlands.

'Anyway, Shirley,' said her friend Mrs Knight, 'you needn't worry. It's the same as last time, the baby will come back as soon as the parents pay up, and it looks as though they can well afford it. The next day the baby will be back safe and sound.'

'You mean this has happened before?' asked Shirley in an appalled voice.

'Considering your father owns this paper you should read it. Yes, don't you remember? A few months ago, I think. These criminals copy each other; that's what publicity does.'

'Oh, it's too awful to think about,' Flora cried in an almost hysterical voice.

'It's all right, Flora, you're not a millionnaire, nobody will want Cherry,' Sarah said meaning to soothe.

'Yes, yes, but there's my Great Uncle Alabaster, the banker. He doesn't give it to us, but he's terribly rich. A kidnapper might think ... Oh God, if Cherry disappeared —' said Flora, by now pale and clutching her bosom. Sarah was reminded of the tug at unaccustomed pectoral nerves that fear induces in lactating women. 'I think about it all the time, I can't stop,' Flora went on. 'That's why I want Cherry near me. Not outside, or anywhere else. It happened, you see, it happened last winter to someone my mother knew. The daughter of one of her friends in the village. Lady Grylls.' All the women in the room must have recognized the name, they looked impressed and Margaret Knox was nodding thoughtfully, for it was one of those which might as well be written with dollar signs. 'Her daughter was staying with her and the baby was stolen, just like that. They'd only gone in for a minute. All gone, the pram and all. Which just shows that it isn't safe to leave a baby, not for a minute. I just daren't.'

'But the baby came back perfectly well,' Margaret Knox said, sounding a little angry.

51

'Yes, I know, but they paid a huge sum and the kidnappers were never caught. The baby was gone for almost a week, imagine what it was like waiting. Jennifer Grylls hasn't ever been the same since.'

Margaret Knox said in a bracing, slightly impatient voice, 'Well, that just shows you. Lightning never strikes twice and all that, so you needn't worry if it happened to a friend of yours.'

'Anyway, Flora, nobody knows that you could touch the Alabaster lolly,' Sarah said, in the encouraging tone of voice she would use to one of her children. Flora was very agitated, and the wide spaced eyes and bulging forehead of an earnest school girl were furrowed and creased with anxiety. 'You would never be expected to have huge ransom sums.'

'No, no, I don't tell *anyone*,' Flora said, to her four listeners.

Shirley Richardson said in a 'let's keep calm' sort of way, 'Why should anyone want to kidnap a baby, do you think, in the first place?'

'Really, ducky!' Her friend looked at her in a sort of despair. One could see, thought Sarah, that Shirley had always been bottom of her class. 'For the money, of course, what else.'

'There must be easier ways of making money,' Shirley said obstinately.

'Can you think of any?' Sarah said, who had often failed to do just that. There was a brief silence as all the women pondered, and then Sarah said, 'You see, there aren't really. Not by honest work, anyway, even if one were qualified to do any, what with income tax and insurance stamps and having a housekeeper.'

'I'd take to a life of crime,' Shirley said enthusiastically. Her plump cheeks shone, and her wiry hair seemed to curl tighter above the birdlike eyes, as she contemplated it.

'Not all that simple,' Sarah said. 'I'm sure you need a gang for safe breaking. Or blackmail, for instance – how do you find out peoples' murky secrets to start with?'

'I'd go on the streets,' Shirley said persistently.

52

'Well, bully for you,' Sarah replied. In fact it was hard to imagine this innocent dumpling of a woman seducing anyone, especially in competition with professionals. Margaret Knox was being neglected in her corner, and Sarah leant towards her to ask what she thought.

'I doubt whether you'd make more than pocket money as a prostitute,' she replied politely. 'After all, this kidnapper is making thousands.'

All the women gave up at this. Sarah was glad that it seemed to be time for them to go; her house became unbearably hot if the sun shone through the picture windows and the architect had not allowed for prevailing winds in designing the openings. In deference to the hairdresser time that her guests had put in, she had chosen that morning to swelter rather than blow away, and was longing for a chance to cool down.

They all gathered round as Flora brought her carrycot down, and admired the baby buried deep in it. Margaret Knox had come with her Mary too, and compared the two with a certain professionalism.

'It's just like the photograph in that paper,' Shirley said laughing, and Mrs Knox agreed.

'Most tiny babies are indistinguishable,' she said. 'See one and you've seen nearly all.'

'Not to their mothers!' This concession to sentimentality agreed, three cars swept out of the close, and Sarah sighed with relief. Flora, however, looked frightened at the prospect of going home. She explained, 'I'm not very keen on the house alone. It still has unfamiliar noises.' So Sarah stood chatting on the doorstep with her for a while, determined not be forced to invite her in again. She had a date, that afternoon, to get to London in time for dinner with Vic. That useful dentist was serving as an excuse again, and on the strength of it Jeffrey had promised to leave the office early enough to fetch Marcus and Emily from school.

'I really will have to go back. I have an awful lot to do, George's socks to darn and so on,' Flora said regretfully.

'Well, that's a waste of time, if you like. Buy him new ones, for goodness sake. They are cheaper than a pair of tights for you.'

'Oh, I don't think he'd like that, any more than he does things like instant mashed potato.'

'Need he know?' Sarah asked, but Flora was shocked at the idea of keeping secrets from him. He seemed, Sarah could only conclude, something of a domestic tyrant, and she could not understand why anybody, nowadays, should be in subjection to one.

'Were you very strictly brought up?' she asked.

'No, my mother was on her own, from the time I was three, so she had to do everything herself. I was a latch-key kid really.'

'No father figure?'

'No, my mother didn't marry again, and there weren't any uncles who took much notice of me. You're probably doing a bit of do-it-yourself psychology, Sarah, I bet you're thinking that explains my marrying George. Though he's only twelve years older than I am, I'm not the fledgling I look.'

'I wasn't —' Sarah started, embarrassed, but Flora interrupted, and said,

'It's all right, I don't mind. What's wrong with my choosing a father figure even if I did? There's nothing against it. It's no more peculiar than an art student falling in love with an artistic architect.'

'Well, one can get jolly sick of the artistic temperament, I can tell you. I wouldn't say no to a bit of fatherly attention these days. Jeffrey's so abstracted he might just as well not be here at all.'

But for the last few weeks Jeffrey might have caught preoccupation from his wife. She organised the household and produced the meals as usual, lay in Jeffrey's arms if he came to bed before two in the morning and happened to notice she was there. Sometimes she would wake with the alarm clock and find his bedside light still burning and a chaste barrier down the middle of the bed of huge volumes about town planning, over which her husband had fallen asleep.

But Sarah's thoughts too were far from home. As she

54

scooted competently round the supermarket, or read boring words aloud, her imagination was enjoying the child-free, elegant world of Vic Nightingale. In her mind's eye she dressed in fashionable clothes and lunched at Claridges, had tea on the terrace of the House of Commons, carried on sparkling conversations or walked silently hand in hand with Victor. She usually stopped short of imagining, or in fact, remembering the private events in his bedroom; for one thing, he was a bit flimsy for her, and for another she really, once she came to think about it, only loved Jeffrey. Anyway, Jeffrey wasn't jealous about her, he'd never notice. Even if he came into the room when she was making love to another man he'd just say 'Sorry' and leave in a hurry. In a way it would be fun to be married to a man who would reach for his gun. Jeffrey would never talk about hypotheses, and just laughed when she asked what he'd do if that happened. Sarah knew fine what she would do herself, grab the children and go home to mum – and never come back. But Jeffrey was not a jealous man, and anyway, bodies weren't all that important. The intimate chats she had – in her imagination, so far – with Vic were far more a betrayal of married privacies than her physical infidelity.

The long unread, dusty volumes of the *Khama Sutra* and do-it-yourself love manuals seemed far more embarrassing now than they had when Sarah read them at the beginning of her sexual career. They had made her feel sexy and enthusiastic then, though fairly soon she and Jeffrey had settled into a happy routine. To visualize performing these contortions now, with one's husband, was very blushmaking, but she didn't want Vic to think she was boring. Nor, the protective thought perhaps slightly misplaced, did she want him to despise her husband for not making sure that his wife knew more sophisticated tricks. Sarah was reminded of an episode two summers ago when they had been on holiday in Ireland; they had shared a cottage with some rather older friends with teenage children, and an engaged couple had come to stay. All the time they had been urging the young people to go off alone together, or making sure that there was a bedroom where they could lock themselves

55

in, for all the world like the pandering madames of some rural brothel. And then one day Sarah and Jeffrey, walking in the heather, had stumbled on their middle-aged, long-married friends making love in a hollow; and all had been hideously embarrassed. It had almost spoilt the rest of the holiday. There was something positively indecent about people who were married making love. It was only acceptable to visualize between the young; which would create problems when it came to explaining the facts of life to the children.

Though Sarah herself was going round in a dream, she resented the fact that Jeffrey was preoccupied. His invincibly sweet temperament made him extremely though absent-mindedly polite, so that Sarah could not even complain that she cooked thanklessly, or spoke unanswered. It was just that he was so often not there; it was so easy for the children's father to escape them.

On Saturday, the day after a rather inconclusive evening at the theatre with Vic during which he had been so nervous as to make her suppose that he was ashamed to be seen with her, Jeffrey pushed cereal packets around at breakfast to plan the relationship of high-rise flats, and having remarked in devoted tones on the children's sweetness and Sarah's sweetness, 'just nipped out to the office'.

'And that's the last we see of him today,' his wife muttered bitterly, watching from the window, and wondering whether the quarrel downstairs would sort itself out if ignored.

It was pouring with rain, as so often in an Orton summer, and Sarah watched Jeffrey hunched into his corduroy jacket as he opened the garage doors, and she almost could hear the raindrops smashing on to the bald circle of his head.

Emily had left her doll's pram outside, and in her present mood Sarah hoped that Jeffrey would run it over. It would serve the child right. But he got out, once the old car was ticking over, and patiently moved it to one side. Overcome with remorse, Sarah rushed to hug her daughter, but Marcus came to join in, each poked the other, and that was the end of the tableau of happy family life.

Sarah, sulkily cooking the inordinate quantities of food which four people seemed to need at a weekend, decided that her only weapon against the *Architectural Review* and the drawing-board was Jeffrey's vanity. She served steamed fish and salad for dinner that evening and announced that unless he took more exercise that would be his everyday diet from then on.

So the next day they set out as a family to Whitfield Park, which was the bolt-hole for the entire population of Orton. On a fine Sunday it was almost standing-room only; the park was full of families in identical chain-store clothes with identical family-sized cars. Sarah wondered where the difference lay between herself and them, but Jeffrey was too un-selfconscious to recognize the likeness. He did all the proper things simply because they were what he wanted to do – explored hollow trees, ate ice-creams and threw bread to ducks. Sarah sat dissociating herself on a bench near the entrance.

Dogs were barking, and ice-cream bells ringing. Children raced and shrieked. It was the sort of noise which, once noticed, is not possible to ignore. Somewhere a very small baby was wailing, and the woman sitting beside Sarah said in a disapproving voice,

'Been there for ages, that poor mite has. The mother didn't ought to leave it like that, it's not right.' Sarah nodded, uninterested, and glanced where the woman was pointing to a cheap folding pram parked by the gate. There did not seem to be anyone in attendance, and when a large dog poked its muzzle curiously into the mound of blankets, the disapproving woman got up briskly and said, 'They ought to get the welfare to that woman. Leaving the baby alone like that.' She marched briskly up to the pram and shooed the dog away. She stood for a moment rocking the handle, and then, looking behind her for an irate mother, stooped to pick up the child. Then she screamed, the piercing note louder than that of the baby in her arm. Her free hand held a piece of paper, and she was shouting something. Sarah strolled over to see what the fuss was about; there was a crowd standing there now, and Sarah could see nothing but a glimpse of fair hair and a pink shawl; but the crowd was passing the news on, and an excited girl turned round to Sarah and said, 'It's the kidnapped baby. Karen Jones. Oh, isn't it marvellous? That note says it is. They've brought her back.'

A police car arrived almost at once, and a young woman in uniform, smiling unprofessionally, carried the baby in her arms into the car. The pram, which looked brand-new, was folded and put into the boot, and as the car drove off one of the crowd called, 'Taking her all the way to London then, are you?' and a dark blue arm waved from the window. The young woman said knowledgeably, 'They're as pleased as anyone, the coppers are. Having the baby delivered back without trouble.'

It was fantastic how policemen and newspapermen could spring up out of the ground. Sarah had seen it happen before, when she was witness once to a road accident. Now, even before Jeffrey returned with the children, the crowd was being cordoned off and questioned by uniformed constables, and the moment the members of it were released they were pounced upon by eager young men with shorthand notebooks. All the questions were the same. Had they seen anyone leave the pram there, had they seen anything suspicious, had they ever seen that pram before; and all were unanswerable, the last particularly so since the pram, in the brief glimpse anyone had seen of it after the excitement, had been a standard, cheap model, manufactured by the million; in any case, in a park on a fine Sunday there must be two thousand prams being unnoticeably pushed or parked, and ten per cent of them were probably identical with the one in which Karen Jones had been found.

There was a knowledgeable woman who was telling anyone who would listen that this was only to be expected. Apparently the last baby to be so spectacularly kidnapped, ransomed and returned had also been found in a brand new pram, with a note pinned to the blanket, and in excellent health. It was, if one came to think of it, a foolproof way for the kidnappers to return the child. Any woman could park a pram without a second glance from anyone else, outside a shop, or, as here, near an ice-cream van which was just outside the park gate. And then she could walk away, taking the additional precaution of removing a wig or head-scarf if she chose. Easy as winking, the knowledgeable woman said.

When Jeffrey and the children came back, much pleased with themselves, Sarah said it was time to go home. But if Jeffrey did a thing at all, he did it properly and he said that it would be nice to drive about a bit. Whitfield Park was about ten miles from Orton, and he was sure there must be some pretty villages in between, if only they turned off the main road. Perhaps Sarah would like to move to a village, he suggested considerately; she might get quite involved with Women's Institutes and things like that.

Sarah thought that the villages they went through were muddy and unenticing, and the red brick houses, like the Minibrick edifices she had built in her nursery, did not appeal. The suburbs were horrid but if one could not live where one wanted to, it made no difference where one was. She solaced her eye with spotting cars like Victor's as though, knight-like, he was coming to bear her away. She saw a similar one parked, but no Vic. Jeffrey continued to point out period gems, the terraces of cottages named after Queen Victoria's children, or the gabled rows of 'Coronation Cottages' which all the Brockshire villages could boast. His enthusiasm became quite unbridled at the sight of an axed railway station in the village of Mirkby. A dark red-brick house, with white-painted wooden fretworks along the roof ridge and above the arched windows; a garden neat with rows of vegetables; a chicken run and a dovecote.

'That's what I mean, darling, d'you see? Come on, let's get out and have a look at this village. It's only in places like this that you find the old traditions – wouldn't you like to live here and have a nice garden and keep hens? We could have our own free-range eggs for breakfast.'

The children, out of the car, were running down the narrow pavement to the railway bridge. At one side of it was a picket fence, and they were craning their heads down

59

to look at the derelict permanent way.

'I'd love to live in a station,' said Jeffrey romantically. 'Think what I could do with it. Such scope for conversion.'

'I don't like it much here,' said Sarah dampeningly. 'It's so flat, and muddy, and it smells of drains. And look how awful the school is, it must have been a workhouse.'

'I still like the station house. Look how lovingly it's kept, and it hasn't been taken over by people like us – it's just a natural, old-fashioned country house.'

Jeffrey had been brought up in Croydon, and his experience of country life was derived from six months at Lark-hill training camp when he was doing National Service – after that he had spent the rest of his time on the Luneberg Heath in North Germany, pining for rural Wiltshire – and from the few novels he had read, when he could spare the time from work. He knew that away from places like Croydon and Orton was the natural world of Old England, with villagers earning honest livings, cultivating their own gardens and downing a pint at the local in the evening. He regularly listened to 'The Archers'.

He gazed at the little house for a while, with Sarah noting its bad points, and saying how dark and poky it must be inside. Probably had no plumbing either. Jeffrey had a rapt expression on his face, and Sarah said spitefully, 'You would only destroy it if you got your mitts on it, my dear. You'd let in the light here and the vista there, and knock out the partition walls and by the time you finished it wouldn't be your little rural residence at all any more, just another piece of copy for the magazines.'

Jeffrey looked injured, and said in a wounded voice, 'Oh, I think I'd keep its character. But never mind, since you aren't interested, let's go home. Where are the children?'

Marcus and Emily had wandered further up the road, and were talking to a tall woman with a basket. Behind them, a tall thin man who reminded Sarah of Vic – but then everything did nowadays – was walking rapidly away.

'There, you see,' said Jeffrey furiously. 'Look how you bring those children up. Is that what you teach them, to talk to strangers? I should have thought even you would have more sense than that.'

Sarah got into the car, hunching her coat around her neck.

'They are your children too,' she pointed out, on the principle that where there was no defence one could only attack. 'Why don't you teach them not to talk to people? I'll tell you why, it's because you're never there, you are becoming a stranger to them. I'll tell you what, Jeffrey —' but Jeffrey had marched crossly off down the street, and came back dragging the howling children. He flung them on to the back seat, and leapt in, but his anger never lasted, and he always disarmed by apologizing.

'I'm sorry, darling,' she said, but Sarah was nursing a grievance, and did not answer. She snapped at Marcus and Emily, 'Oh, do shut up,' and Marcus wailed.

'It was Margaret, Mummy, that lady we was talking to, Margaret that comes to see us at home, the baby lady, why was Daddy so cross?'

'Daddy was beastly to be cross, wasn't he?' Sarah agreed. She handed the children a sweet each, and said, 'Never mind, forget it now.'

'But it *was* Margaret, Mum,' Marcus insisted, and Sarah craned her neck around, but the woman was out of sight. If it had been a stranger, the children were naughty to speak to her, goodness knows how often she had told them not to, but it was not fair for Jeffrey to leave the children entirely to her and then interfere so capriciously. She would scold them, later, and explain about nasty men, but not when Jeffrey could hear her. She didn't want him to know that she was admitting to being in the wrong.

VIII

'My dearest Victor,' the letter began. Gordon Buddle pursed his lips in a subsónic whistle. 'How glad I am to offer another contribution. I do look forward to seeing you,

61

and shall give it to you when we meet, with discretion as usual. I wish it were even more. Surely it won't be too long now before the fund is big enough at least for a beginning.

'I wish you would answer my question about the possible addition to the band of workers. I have tried – as tactfully as I can, without giving a thing away – to decide what you would feel about it. It seems to me that there is perhaps too much levity there, and too much interest in matters of no importance. But I know you are still undecided. Do reassure me, when I see you. One or two remarks have made me wonder whether your motives are indeed what I thought in this case. But I know that such suspicion is unworthy. My faith in you is still unbounded. I long for the day when I shall be proved right. Your devoted.'

The signature was a squiggle of initial at the end of the typed page. Buddle had been taught, on the crash course which his second employers had laid on, that a person who made a twist of indecipherable handwriting for his signature was full of vanity or inferiority complex. Like various other such hallmarks – for example, that a full mouth denoted generosity, or that very blue eyes indicated sexiness – he took this lesson with a large pinch of doubt. After all, he had a full mouth and blue eyes himself. In any case, vanity and inferiority were not homing beams which would help him track the writer of this letter down. He would make a bet that the writer was a woman, but that did not get him very much further either.

He took a quick shot of the letter, before resealing it in the chain-store envelope. The paper was so cheap that the steam had wrinkled it, but he had just time to iron it flat before laying it at the bottom of the pile. In a way it hurt his professional pride to be reduced to such schoolboy tricks as steaming letters open. He had managed his last job far more neatly. But Vic Nightingale, blast him, was excessively careful about taking the few letters Buddle needed to see away with him, envelopes and all, as though Buddle might not have noticed that they existed at all. But then he wasn't used to servants, hadn't been brought up to them.

Even if there had not been another reason for doing so, Buddle would have made sure he knew what went into that breakfast-table letter pile.

The camera was a nice toy, though. He hoped he'd be able to keep that. Had more uses than letters, after all. Just right for a breast pocket, it was. He patted the little instrument affectionately as he stowed it away under the Paisley silk handkerchief. At least the job had some perks.

He showed Folly Armitage the results; not that he told her about it of course, he copied out the words of the letter from the print in longhand and that was all she got to see. But she was fast enough at working things out if she was keen. Odd girl, really, he thought, not for the first time. She hadn't been lying when she said she wasn't interested in much. A real monomaniac she was, what they used to call a one-track mind. Didn't give an instant's thought to anything else, just baled out her mind like a leaky boat if he mentioned anything that she thought was irrelevant. But the letter was a big catch.

'A woman,' she said at once. 'Nobody else would gush like that. Unless it's an old queer – oh, I beg your pardon, Gordon. But I don't think so. It strikes a motherly note to me. I suppose it's not from his mother?'

'It says in *Who's Who*, miss, that he's an orphan.'

'Yes, that's what he told me. I suppose it might be true. An aged aunt or something?'

'You'd know more about his family than I do, if you're his fiancee.'

'I'm not quite that yet, as you know very well. I certainly haven't been taken home to meet the family. I suppose they live in a slum or something. I know he's the poor boy made good.'

'He went to school in Ferraby, miss.'

'Yes, and to the university afterwards. I never knew there was a university there till I met Vic.'

'A women he met when he was there perhaps? Some elderly admirer, like a lecturer or something?'

'Could be. I've half a mind to go down there and scout around. It's one of those hideous places one drives through

63

on the way north. It's got one of those bypasses that take you all the way round the church and up the steeple, through the slums. Shall I go and have a look at it? At least the motorway goes near by.'

'Yes, why don't you do that, Miss Armitage?' Buddle agreed. Keep her out of mischief for a bit, that would. He had other ways of going about things himself. He sped Folly Armitage on her way with polite good wishes, and she promised to let him know how she got on. He didn't tell her that there was no need to do this. He had every intention of following her progress himself. As he went upstairs to change, he was humming the tune of Loch Lomond. But Folly Armitage was singing at the top of her voice, attracting stares from the rush-hour drivers. And her song was 'I'm getting married in the morning'.

IX

Sarah could hardly refuse to look after the baby on Tuesday. Flora Millington appeared on the doorstep, with the baby ready dressed for visiting, a bag of nappies at her feet and a confident and grateful smile on her face. It was nothing serious, she hastened to assure Sarah, only a bit of tidying up to do, a scrape or a stitch, or something. But the bed had come up and the hospital would not promise another if she missed the chance; it seemed rather convenient in a way, while George was away, because he always got so upset when she was laid up and he'd had a lot of it recently. So could Sarah possibly? Just a couple of days, and after all, it was not as though Cherry was a troublesome baby. In fact it would be nice for Sarah to have a baby in the house again. Flora looked fondly at the sleeping child, and with a smile which she intended to convey reproach Sarah carried the cot into the house. Flora's thanks were grateful but not effusive, and it became plain that she had not doubted that Sarah would take over, when an ambulance appeared on the dot of ten o'clock and with great composure Flora climbed in beside the two elderly patients and a couple of heavily pregnant women.

Sarah left the baby crying for food, and went back furiously to her interrupted task: she was decorating her face with unaccustomed elaboration. Two layers of foundation cream blended on her skin, powder blotted on and set with cold water, eye make-up painted with a series of tiny brushes, no fewer than four layers of lipstick. Sarah was dredging from her memory the advice given in magazines, and in the pages of her mind she could still see the photographs of models before, during and after the beautifying process. She knew, she thought, how it should be. And a little later wondered whether she had overdone it.

She went down in her petticoat to feed the child, forcing herself to patience in warming and then cooling the milk, in patting the back and rubbing the stomach, the hateful task of washing the bottom and powdering the creases. It seemed worth doing it properly in the hope that the incubus would sleep. A baby in the back of the car was one thing, but a screaming baby on the knees was another, and she would not have her day ruined by it.

For Sarah had a rendezvous in the motorway cafe with Vic, and she was damned if Flora's blasted baby would prevent her keeping it. Marcus and Emily, after all, had been taken everywhere with her when they were babies, they had lived their lives in the back of the car, and had made themselves useful into the bargain, disarming policemen and traffic wardens. It would do Cherry no harm; though Sarah hoped that nobody would look at her and suppose that she belonged to Sarah. She had always been rather proud of her own babies, but Cherry was unattractive, hairless and round and without any particular distinction. Just a baby like thousands of others; Marcus and Emily had been unmistakable.

It took her a long time to decide what to wear, for she was not sure what convincing reason she could give Vic for just happening to be able to meet him there and then. She certainly did not want him to suppose that she would drive thirty miles each way to a dismal cafe just to see him. Was she on her way to or from London? In that case, the black dress would be best. But it creased so if worn for driving. Or perhaps an antique sale somewhere in Bucks. That sounded both likely and suitable, and Sarah pulled out a trouser suit from the cupboard. It was important to make the right impression on him.

The carrycot fitted familiarly in the back of the car but Sarah felt irritation at the remembered demands of small babies rather than the broody nostalgia which they had induced in her the year before. A love-affair was a marvellous substitute for breeding as a time-filler. Cherry was soothed by the journey and fast asleep when Sarah pulled in at the motorway car park and stopped between a Rolls and a van. She left the quarter light open, and put on the theft lock which Jeffrey had insisted on buying; of course the tail gate would not lock any more, but the car was now unstealable, and quite apart from that precaution, she had always felt confident that nobody would steal a car with a baby in it. Car thieves after all were relatively unpersecuted, whereas baby thieves had every man's hand against them. Sarah stubbornly continued to believe that the kidnapping of the pop-singer's baby augured no danger to her own poor children.

She looked warily around as she approached the cafe, but saw nobody she knew; Vic was going north, so she crossed over the glass bridge, pausing to look down at the terrifying traffic. When one saw the motorway from the outside it was remarkable that anyone dared to venture on it. The grey van she had parked beside was drawing out, for her visual memory recognised the number plate; it was being driven by a woman who looked like Margaret Knox, but her car was a blue Morris. It would be an odd coincidence though, especially since it was through her that Sarah had encountered Vic.

Vic was fiddling with slimy sandwiches at a dirty table and looked more at home than Sarah liked to imagine herself in such surroundings. He greeted her without effusion, without even his usual polite cheek to cheek, which

66

would perhaps have been too noticeable here, but apart from such precaution Sarah thought that he looked worried.

'Anything wrong?' she said lightly.

'No, no, not at all. Lovely to see you. What luck that we could meet here. Where are you off to?'

'A sale further south.'

'Oh, do you collect furniture?' For a moment it seemed strange that Vic should know so little about the way she lived, but Sarah hastily reminded herself what an arrangement of convenience theirs was and answered civilly.

But after a while Sarah felt a creeping depression and disappointment and realized that her journey had not been worth the effort; Vic was glancing at his watch, and his replies to her conversation were not products of the concentration with which he usually flattered those to whom he talked. She realized that what was an exciting and rather naughty outing for her was a time-consuming engagement dutifully undertaken in the middle of a busy day for Vic. She thought, 'I know when I'm not wanted', and said lightly:

'I must get a move on, I've left a baby in the car.'

'Oh, one of yours?'

'No, Vic, I've told you that my younger one is nearly six. It's a neighbour's baby I'm minding.'

'Neglecting?'

'Well, perhaps. But I always left my own babies in the car.' She began to feel guilty at this suggestion, and wondered whether risks one might permissibly take with one's own belongings were unjustified with someone else's. She quickened her step across the bridge and felt positively relieved to be able to see her own car still parked where she had left it. She said:

'There's no need to see me to my car if you're in a hurry.'

'Oh, well, perhaps – if you don't mind. I must just buy a paper and so on – lovely to see you, what a lucky coincidence we were both passing.' He patted her on the shoulder and turned back to the northbound side.

There was no sound of crying coming from the car, and

67

Sarah had unlocked the driving door and chucked her bag in before she glanced back to check on the baby.

The carrycot was empty, the blankets thrown back and white sheet unoccupied.

Sarah's body reacted to the shock more quickly than her mind. She was crouched on the driving seat, feet splayed out on the puddled tarmac, heart pounding and breath gasping before, with her brain, she realized what had happened. She was talking aloud – 'Oh my God, oh my God, what shall I do?' She stood up and started to run unsteadily like a drunken woman, tripping over loose stones and blinded by her hair. It felt as though her legs were weighted down by boulders. But there was nobody to help her. The girls in the sweet kiosk stared with vacant eyes, their cud-chewing unperturbed; the garage man was a Jamaican who did not understand her English. She stumbled up the steps, across, down the steps, out into the car park on the other side. There were groups of travellers in the way, she was muttering 'Get out of my way, damn you, get out of my way.' But Victor's car was not in the car park. She wasted several minutes searching for it before the part of her mind that was still working told her that he would have gone by now. She started to run back up, over and down, not really believing that it could be true. The people standing around were watching her now and laughs followed her but no help was offered and she could not see anybody suitable to ask for it. There were no police cars and there were bovine queues outside the telephone kiosks.

The baby had not miraculously returned.

She leapt into the car and roared out of the park. She was trembling all over, but she felt, as she did when slightly drunk, more than usually in control of her machinery. She wove her way between the dithering vehicles and forced her way out on to the motorway. Reckless now, she glanced in the wing mirror to see that it was momentarily clear of following traffic and turned her car straight at the central reservation. The northbound carriageway was crowded and everybody passed her with long wailing hoots and glaring headlights, but she completed the U-turn and started to drive north; she placed herself in the outside lane and stayed there. The wheel alignment of her car needed attention, and when she drove above 65 miles an hour the steering-wheel juddered and leapt in her hand, but she forced her right foot flat on to the floor and rode the machine braced like a steeplechaser. At first she would have been glad to be stopped by the police, and thought, in so far as she could think straight, that she would have welcomed their attentions. But she realized pretty quickly that she dared not tell them of Cherry's disappearance for they would instantly inform the child's mother; and Sarah did not dare to think of Flora hearing this news. Somehow, God knows how, she must cope with this disaster alone. A vision of the empty cot kept leaping between Sarah and the road but she blinked and persevered. She knew that Vic was a stickler for speed limits, having a lively sense of preserving himself from the wrong kind of publicity; if she kept the needle wavering at eighty, somehow, somewhere, she should overtake him. With tears, hair and visions impeding her sight, she blinded on along the busy road.

Sarah's driving was crazy enough for her to catch up with Vic but her gestures did not persuade him to stop and she had not, even in this emergency, the nerve to force him on to the hard shoulder at the side of the road. He looked at her with fury as she hooted and waved, and he swerved his car away from her like a dodging footballer, when she steered close to him. He pulled off the road at the next sliproad after she caught up with him and sat waiting for her grimly in the nearest lay-by. He snapped that she deserved to be whisked off to the nearest police station, but she had not time for apologies.

'Vic, you must help me – I didn't know what to do, there wasn't anyone to ask – it's so dreadful – all I could think of was to catch up with you.'

Victor Nightingale's features grew suddenly weasely and suspicious as he realized that Sarah was determined to involve him in something certainly tiresome and possibly compromising.

'It's the baby, Vic, Flora's baby. I had her in the car, I

69

left her while I came to meet you, I always used to leave Marcus and Emily, it was always perfectly safe, I never thought anything would happen, but now someone's taken Cherry and I don't know what to do.'

'Taken the baby? How do you mean?'

'Look!' Sarah flung open the tail gate of her car and displayed the empty cot. Vic looked at it crossly, and leant in to pick up a brown envelope which Sarah had not seen tucked under the frilled pillow. Sarah snatched it from him and tore it open.

Inside was a sheet of typing paper with a carbon typed message. There were spaces left in a few places, which had been filled in with a childish, backward leaning handwriting, in blue ballpoint pen. It read,

'You will get your baby back perfectly safe and happy if you follow these instructions. You must raise enough money to buy ten solitaire diamond rings with a resale value of £500 each. Put them into the (bag) and (leave it on the floor in the third lavatory cubicle on the right as you go into the ladies' cloakroom at this service station.) If you do not enable me to collect this undetected you can guess what my next step will be. But nobody has dared to test it so far.' (The words in brackets were those filled in by hand.) There was a paper clip attaching a few papers to the message; they included a small brown paper bag on which was printed in blue 'Sanitary Bag for use in Ladies' Lavatories', and a tear in the corner showed where it had been detached from the string which looped a pile of these bags to the back of a lavatory door. And there were cuttings from newspapers which described the kidnapping of small babies; one was called Arabella Grylls, the other Karen Jones. Two others showed photographs of the weeping mothers reunited with their babies. The legend read in each case that the ransom had been paid, and the baby had been found in good health, once outside a shop, once at Whitfield Park, with a note saying who the child was pinned to the underside of the blanket.

Sarah could not believe that she was reading accurately the expression on Vic's face. But a dispassionate observer

70

would have said that he was furious. He wanted out.

'There really isn't anything I can do about this, Sarah. You had better get hold of the child's mother and the police and leave it in their hands. I can't help you.'

'But you must. Really, I can't cope.' Sarah heard her voice coming out high and whining, like a child on the verge of tears. Only a day before one of her fantasies centred on Vic had been herself in despair; wounded in not too unglamorous a part of her body, bravely bearing the pain as Vic wiped her tears away. It had never been one of her best fantasies, for there was no doubt that being with Victor would be more fun if one were whole and free, and even when inventing episodes which one really never desired to happen it was impossible to forget certain inconvenient facts; like, for example, that Sarah knew she looked hideous when crying, or when pale from illness. So she took a couple of deep breaths and tried to produce an unshaking voice from somewhere below the tonsils. But her throat felt as though it were aching with the effort and she could only speak in a tightly controlled murmur, if she were not to abandon herself to hysteria.

'Look, Vic, I can't tell the child's mother, I can't let her discover about it at all. I was responsible for the baby, can you imagine what she would think? And she's in hospital. Anyway, she hasn't been well since Cherry was born, I don't think she's very stable. God knows what this would do to her, it might send her crazy. There must be some way of getting Cherry back before Flora knows about this. But I haven't any money, not a bean. How could I spend £5000 on diamond rings?'

'You'd better tell the police, then.'

'But they'd tell Flora at once, and get her husband back. They'd have to ask her to find out where he is, it's somewhere in Finland, I think. I can't, Vic, don't you see?'

Vic said, 'Can't you raise some money? Most people have a car or a house they could sell, if it's desperate.'

'But it's all Jeffrey's.' Sarah looked at Vic's hostile face. How could she have had amorous fantasies about a man with such small bones, such a lipless slit where Jeffrey had a generous full mouth? His eyes were darting about, never meeting hers, and he dangled his bunch of keys suggestively, to show that any minute now he intended to drive away. He looked ostentatiously at his watch. She thought, this is my last resort, and said desperately,

'Vic, listen to me. I'll tell you in words of one syllable. There's plenty of evidence, even if it's only circumstantial, that you have been having an affair with me. Jeffrey would divorce me for it. That wouldn't help your famous career. If you don't help me get out of this mess it's you that will suffer.'

'Are you threatening me?'

'I suppose I am, in a way. And I may say that I'm pretty surprised at your attitude. Why aren't you thinking about that poor little baby? I thought you were the one who's supposed to be so full of compassion and sympathy. Don't look now but your image is slipping.'

'Anyway, what do you think I can do?'

'Just be a bit helpful, for a start. But couldn't you raise some money? You must be rolling, and you ought to feel responsible because I'd never have been there at all but for coming to meet you. Cherry would be safely at home.'

'I knew you'd come there just to meet me.' For an instant, his face melted from distaste to complacency.

'You can forget that now. What about the money?' Sarah sank down on to the roadside verge, squatting on her heels. She felt as though she could not go on fighting with Victor. It was so dreadful to have to. But she would not think about that now.

Victor was chewing at the skin on his thumb. He looked down at her and said:

'I haven't got any money either. That's just the trouble. I've had very heavy expenses recently, in fact I've been trying to get hold of some more to tide me over. But I – well, I live above my means, you know.'

'But you've got a house, and a car, and all that. Surely you could raise a lot.'

'The house has a hundred per cent mortgage from the GLC. The car – well, I've only paid about an eighth of its

72

price so far. And it may be an expensive one —' his eye momentarily caressed the sparkling silver metal – 'but I couldn't raise more than a hundred quid on it at the moment. And my income is completely spoken for. I should think that my manservant is better off than I am.'

'Well, where were you going to get hold of more and how much will it be?'

'That's a rather bizarre aspect of the affair. I'm hoping for just about four or five thousand to tide me over. But it's to pay a debt, I'm afraid. The money won't be mine to use.'

Sarah thought, he's nothing but a con man really. But that was something else to save for thinking about another time. She said suddenly,

'Why did you want to have an affair with me anyway?'

'Just for fun. Wasn't it fun?'

'You never wanted to get landed with me for keeps?'

'Well, Sarah, you're married, and there's my constituency, and the Party, and then Folly, you know . . .'

'I quite understand.' The ache had gone from her throat now, and her voice came out calm and even amused. 'So it's all the more important to clear this up and get away. A news item wouldn't help.'

'No, indeed.' His voice was pious about that.

Sarah looked at the time; Marcus and Emily would be coming out of school in two and a half hours; but Flora was incarcerated until Friday, and nobody else knew that Sarah was supposed to be looking after the baby. That gave them three days to get her back. It wasn't much, if one didn't know how to begin.

'I must get back,' she said.

'And I'd better ring my agent.'

'You mean that you'll help me?'

'I don't see what else I can do. I certainly haven't any cash, and it doesn't look as though you have. But God knows where we'll start. Pity we haven't got a tame policeman.'

It was a great relief to be able to stop fighting with Vic. For a moment Sarah felt quite affectionate towards him again. But she reminded herself that his conversion might not last; a few scattered references to publicity and divorce courts would not come amiss.

They got into their respective cars and drove off. Vic's tail lights disappeared round the bends unattainable distances away; on bending roads Sarah's ability, and her car, could not keep up. She feared that he was escaping from her, and started to frame the words of tip-offs to the papers in her mind. Vic would not be allowed to get away with it. But his car waited to follow her through the maze of Orton suburbs, and he came into her house obediently enough.

The commitment to so bizarre a search with an unwilling ally was something Sarah was determined to avoid considering. She realized that she would collapse into despair if she let her mind dwell on the situation. She wondered how she would have felt if it had been her own baby; and was horrified to realize that she would have minded less. At least there would have been nobody else to blame her. She could have paid up or refused to pay up as she thought best; and as Jeffrey thought best. She banished the thought of him too. Vic was no satisfactory substitute, nor ever had been. Though, as she said aloud:

'At least you're some sort of man of action, Vic.'

He looked up, a little surprised, from the paper on which he was doodling. His doodles took the form of intertwined capital letters in a small backward sloping handwriting. Sarah, who had the large black scrawl of an art student, despised it, and the purple ink he affected.

'Even if I were a man of action, which I deny, I have no idea what action to take now.'

Sarah looked round the room in a sort of controlled despair. Victor had been making remarks to that effect ever since they sat down together. She said:

'Well, I've thought of one thing. He or she must have come down the Southbound carriageway to have parked in that car park, and be coming from or going to a place which isn't too far away. They'd have to get back to base quickish because they wouldn't dare to go and buy bottles and all the other paraphernalia, in case we had let there be a publicity splash. And they couldn't rely on the baby having been fed recently. So they must have had baby equipment waiting at home.'

'Well, one couldn't be sure. But I suppose you might be right. Do babies need much equipment though? I believe you if you say so.'

'Yes, they do. And I'll tell you something else, they didn't take the carrycot. That must mean that either there were two people so that one could hold the baby, or they had a sort of cot in their car already. So it would have to be a van, because it would look so suspicious to have a baby loose on the back seat, and it would have looked suspicious before to have an empty cot waiting.'

'You mean you think this was all planned? But how could anybody have known that you would turn up in that car park with a baby?'

'It must have been unpremeditated. An impulse buy, by somebody who had a full purse with her by chance. But from those cuttings whoever does this goes in for it professionally. A steady source of income.'

'Jolly peculiar coincidence that put that impulse buyer right beside a baby which you left alone in an unlocked car,' he said sourly.

'I know it's my fault, Vic. We can talk about that when we've got the baby back. If you ever want to talk to me again, that is.'

'Oh, of course,' he muttered, flashing his political smile.

'You know, Vic, I've just thought of something. It would have to be someone who parked in that huge car park right beside me. Otherwise they'd never have seen the baby; and nobody would dare carry a small baby a long way from one car to another there. I might have come back in the middle.'

'Unless they had seen you going along the up-and-over glass passage.'

Sarah sat silent for a moment, watching in the film of her mind herself walking over there to meet Vic; she had gone with conscious dignity, sucking her stomach in and stroking back her hair with two fingers as provocatively as she knew how, in case he was watching her. She remembered how she had glanced backwards and down to where she had left her car.

'Hey, wait a minute, Vic,' she said suddenly. 'Vic, listen. I saw who was parked beside me and drove away when I was coming over. And it was someone with a van. And what's more, Vic, I know who it is. It's a woman who keeps babies in the house!'

X

Sylvia White had been having a ladies' luncheon party in her house, Vichysoisse and Dover sole, chocolate souffle and peppermint creams. Mrs Romer had come in to clear away, and now the half dozen well-dressed ladies were drinking coffee in the lounge.

'Gorgeous roses, Sylvia,' said Mary MacMaster, gesturing at the flawless border.

'But they don't smell, dear,' Olive James said kindly. 'Queen Elizabeth, they're called; just like frozen vegetables, beautiful to look at and tasteless.'

The sweetcorn with lunch had been out of the deep freeze and Sylvia White had taken some pains with her roses; she was very proud of the bright pink decoration which reappeared every year. She leant forward with a pained smile, but before she could speak caught sight of a small van whisking round into the Knoxs' drive. She sprang to her feet.

'There it is, d'you see? I told you so, I said it would come back!'

'What's that, dear?'

'The van from that babies' home, the one that brings her those babies. I told you about it, it will send me demented. And now it's back again, just when I thought I'd have some peace.'

Mrs White's friends had all heard about the next door

76

babies *ad nauseam*. They had been introduced with the soup and lasted until the subject was brutally changed by Mrs James with the pudding. And they had all been told about it before. With the firmness of a practised committee woman Mrs James drowned her hostess's remarks with a pronouncement about the local theatre, and the other ladies were eager to join in. But the party had been spoilt for Mrs White. She kept thinking of herself tossing and turning all night as the baby broadcast its shrieks through a healthily open window, of the unkindness and lack of consideration of people who were supposed to be her friends. Her small mouth drooped at the corners, and she felt that her eyes were mournful. To Mrs James, she looked sulky, and she found herself thinking that poor Sylvia was getting old. She turned to her and said something practised and kind about the absent son, but Sylvia replied listlessly – though she was usually pleased enough to boast about the boy – and very soon the party broke up. Sylvia waved politely and mechanically until the last car turned the corner. Then she walked, feigning casualness, towards her neighbour's house.

The grey van had not been driven away yet, she had kept a sharp eye open to make sure. Perhaps if one went to call, quite informally, with a good excuse? It might be possible to meet the driver of the van, even to get her alone.

Mrs White hurried into her kitchen and seized a pot of marmalade which Mary MacMaster had given her last autumn. Or no, that wouldn't do. It was the wrong time of year for marmalade. There were two other more seasonal pots; she never ate sweet things, but her friends all had this obsession about jam-making. They didn't eat it either, of course, because of calories, and were obliged to make seasonal gifts to all and sundry. Mrs White, who thought of herself as a realist, considered this process an atavistic ritual designed to show that one had not been rendered unfeminine by emancipation. The only part she took was to accept the end products. So now she chose a jar of lemon curd, hastily wrapped it in the tissue paper which the Spanish Sauternes at lunch had come in, and went out to the next-door house.

It was one of the few houses in the street which had some privacy about it. Most of the others were free standing with their gardens going all round, so that you could never be sure at the back that a curious visitor might not come upon you unexpectedly. And the local style was for picture windows, sometimes net curtained, but usually affording a good view of the modern furniture drawn up around the television set and the lavishly equipped cocktail cabinet. As a matter of fact, there was hardly ever anybody walking down the road to look in. All the residents drove wherever they went – some of the smaller houses used the space on their quarter-acre plots for four and five car garages – and the road was not on the way to anywhere. Sylvia White had sometimes written to Sebastian that she could lie dying for days without anybody noticing anything wrong. She liked the idea that he might be anxious about her, so long as he did not come home and try to do something about it.

The Knoxs' house was unusual in that with its sheds and garage and screening walls it spread from hedge to hedge. All the visible windows were dimmed by net curtains too, and the front door was a solid block of wood, unlike the next-door houses, which had modern glass doors, giving on to porches furnished with blanket chests and rubber plants.

This house was almost barricaded, Sylvia White thought as she walked softly up the short drive. One could not drive straight into the garage, for as well as the five-barred gate on to the pavement, open now, there was a folding door in a sort of wooden wall, which divided off a small yard outside the kitchen door, where dustbins were kept. Beyond that again was the garage, an old brick one built on to the house, with a loft above and a weathercock on the roof ridge.

The folding door was locked; it had an iron circular handle which turned but did not lift the latch. So Mrs White stepped to her left and rang the bell, holding the jar of lemon curd in front of her to avert suspicion from her errand.

Mrs Knox looked flustered when she opened the door to Sylvia White, and smoothed her hair down with her hands as she led her way to the front room. This room had the air of one in which nobody lived; there were neither knitting nor books lying around nor even a television set, though Mrs Knox hastily put a pipe away in a drawer. 'Men make such a mess, don't they,' she remarked, and thereby horrified her visitor, who having spent her life scratching at her ineffectual husband and her unresponsive son, still believed that she had been born to be their handmaiden.

It seemed impossible to ask straight out about the newly arrived baby, or to ask to meet the woman who had brought it. Where was she anyway? Mrs Knox had sat down on the edge of a chair, holding the lemon curd jar on her knee, and made no conversational advances or offers of coffee. But Sylvia settled back on the ugly sofa, and with a polite mutter lit herself a cigarette. There were no ash trays, and Mrs Knox made no move to get one even when Mrs White looked meaningly around, and finally tipped the ash into her own cigarette case.

But Sylvia was rarely at a loss for polite chatter, even when it was to somebody as unresponsive as Mrs Knox, and she passed quickly over the reasons for her visit, mentioning how rarely one managed to meet one's neighbours in this motorized age, how hot it had been, how lovely the roses were this year and so on. It would normally have been disheartening to visit a person who was so obviously longing for one's departure, she thought, but persistence was all. Odd that she couldn't hear anything else in the house. The baby must be up there, now, and the other woman ought to make some sound, it wasn't as though these houses were all that solid.

Having exhausted domestic topics, her eye fell on the pile of weekly papers in a rose-decorated magazine stand. Extraordinary that there were so many, the Knox family must be very well informed, there seemed to be copies of all the political weeklies which Sylvia herself liked to pretend to read and many others, of all shades of opinion. She made some banal remark about the last evening's television news and was surprised that this was the first topic she had tried which made any impression. Mrs White had made a statement which came as naturally to her as saying please and thank you, that the country was going to the dogs. She received a vigorous answer.

'You're absolutely right. It gets worse and worse, with the incompetent self-seekers we have governing us. Old, tired, useless men. What this country needs is a dictator.' She looked ardent and excited, and though never handsome, at least for the first time, alive. Mrs White was not very interested in politics but when she thought of them, had always assumed that all her neighbours would naturally vote as she did.

'Oh, but the last election ... now that we have the government the country needs ...'

'All two-faced self-seekers. Dishonest, power-hungry, incompetent. The whole system's rotten.'

'Really —' Mrs White laughed a little nervously – 'you're very sweeping. Don't you think you go too far? Our system may not be perfect, but in a democracy —'

'Perfect? It's a calamity, all the names and systems and ideologies and rules. One man with vision, with foresight and powers of persuasion, one man to unite all these quarrelling factions and end all their futile arguments.'

'But where will we find a man like that? They don't exist.'

'Oh, at least one does – must exist. But he'll have to beat the system, which takes time, and perseverence, and secrecy. To wait the right moment, that's the problem, to build up strength, conserve resources; and money, of course. It doesn't need a great amount, one wouldn't have to have millions. But enough to keep going, and build up support, until the great moment.'

Mrs White was not of a critical or analytical frame of mind, but some of the phrases which Mrs Knox poured so eagerly forth sounded a little familiar. But Messianic aspirations, like all other political and religious theories, were of no interest to her. She asked, bored:

'Have you got any one in mind?' Mrs Knox had been gazing into the middle distance, but now she turned sharply towards Sylvia and said, 'Of course I haven't. I? Ha, ha!' She laughed unconvincingly.

I think she's mental, Sylvia thought. Shutting herself up here like a hermit, brooding over those blasted babies. And then the happy thought struck her that if she could convince the authorities that Mrs Knox was unstable they might stop her fostering babies altogether. She said, cooing:

'And have you got a little visitor at the moment? I thought I saw one arriving.'

'Oh, did you?'

'Yes, such an old nosy, aren't I? But you can't help seeing things sometimes from my drawing-room. Not that I spy, naturally.'

'No.'

'Don't you ever get nervous, all alone in this big house? I sometimes think that we two lonely women should keep each other company sometimes. And keep an eye out. Don't you ever think that a burglar might come in and leave you for dead and nobody any the wiser? After all, your husband is at home very little, isn't he, dear?'

'He is only here at weekends.'

'I've never been quite sure what he does?'

'He's an agent for the foreign sales of Boot's Fashion (Orton) Ltd. They make ladies' clothes, and export all over the world. But I'm not lonely, I'm quite happy on my own. And now, Mrs White, if you'll excuse —' she stood up, but before finishing her sentence the door bell rang, and seizing her chance, Mrs White said,

'Do answer it. I must just go to the – upstairs, is it?' and she was round the bend of the stairs before Mrs Knox reached the front door. She knew, in fact, where the bathroom must be, for its frosted glass window was visible from her own house, but all the doors on the landing were closed, and she went first to open those on the other side. She was disappointed not to find the uniformed woman from the Mary and Martha Maternity Home in any of the rooms. They were all very conventionally furnished; a spare bedroom with light oak furniture and a yellow candlewick bedspread; a small study, neat and functional and as impersonal as a public lavatory, with a filing cabinet, a modern office desk, and an in-and-out tray. No photographs, no books, no papers lying around. Mrs Knox's own bedroom was furnished in lilac coloured satin, with a frilled valence around the bed and the dressing table. It was a surprise to see a couple of wig stands on a shelf inside the cupboard whose door was swinging open, for Sylvia would never have thought that Mrs Knox was that sort of woman. One of them was empty, and on the other was a draped wig which showed dark through the chiffon scarf over it. The fourth room was the nursery, which Sylvia had been shown on her first visit to the house. There was a baby asleep in the cot, and the usual sour and powdery smell of small babies.

The voices from the door were coming into the hall and Sylvia White nipped in to pull the lavatory chain, and emerged from the bathroom just as Mrs Knox reached the top of the stairs followed by a woman carrying a briefcase.

'Miss Cowan has come to make her routine visit,' Mrs Knox said.

'Yes, we like to check up on registered foster homes,' the young woman agreed, smiling warmly. 'Not that there's any need here, of course, yours is always perfect, Mrs Knox. I only wish we had more like you.'

She opened the door into the nursery and the other two women followed her in. The baby, a tiny creature which could not have been more than three or four weeks old, was whimpering, and Mrs Knox picked it up and patted its back.

Miss Cowan was walking round the room with a pretty mixture of non-interfering shyness and observation. She paused by the trolley, which was piled with folded nappies, opened a drawer to reveal a heap of nightgowns in various colours, and glanced at the mantelpiece, where baby oil, powder, cream, aspirin, gripe water, rose hip syrup and everything else a baby could conceivably need were arranged. She picked up a small bottle and said,

'Phenobarb?'

'Oh, that's mine,' Mrs Knox replied. 'I don't think this little scrap's old enough to get at medicines, do you?'

82

'No, you needn't be locking the bathroom cupboard yet awhile,' she agreed.

'I only wish I could keep them till it was necessary,' said Mrs Knox. 'But they don't stay long enough for that!'

'Well, all I can say is that it's very valuable work. Look how happy this poppet is. But of course you're not working for us just now, are you?'

'No, she comes from my private clients.'

'Dear little creature. Oh well, I'd better be getting on to houses which need my supervision more than you do.'

Sylvia White followed them downstairs turning phrases over in her mind whereby she could persuade the visitor that this was the last place where babies should be housed.

And why hadn't the woman who delivered the child in the first place put in an appearance? She was still baffled as Miss Cowan said a warm goodbye to Mrs Knox, and she hastily followed her out on to the pavement. Mrs Knox shut the door on her goodbyes; anxious to be rid of her, it seemed.

'The babies do cry a good deal,' said Sylvia.

'Oh yes, it's dreadful with small babies, isn't it? Sometimes they make you feel that they're furious at having been brought into this wicked world. It's the feeding, I think, though I wouldn't say so to my clients. They don't get cuddled with the bottle by foster mothers as much as they like, but they get over it. And I must say, Mrs Knox gives them the best start that they could have.'

The young woman fitted herself into a tiny car with the same precision of movement that showed in all her actions. A smile appeared on her face as she looked up at Mrs White, precisely calculated to have the right quantity of friendliness and haste.

'I must get on, I'm behind schedule. Goodbye. Let me know if you think of taking a baby on!' This last was presumably intended as a joke. Mrs White stood on the pavement, between her house and the Knoxs', and forced herself to uncurl her rigid fists, and breathe more calmly. Should she get on to the estate agents and just move straight out?

It was maddening that she had failed to find the driver of

the small grey van in the house; surely all that was needed was a sensible complaint and explanation to her. But there simply must be something she could do.

XI

Sarah had the greatest difficulty in persuading Vic that her idea was remotely sensible. In fact he thought she was out of her mind.

'It's a waste of time you know. It's a wild goose chase. There's just nothing other than coincidence to link this poor woman with the baby. I think it's time to call the police. Though God knows how you'll explain why you didn't do it before.'

'Why *we* didn't, you mean.' In a curious way, the continuous sparring with Victor was keeping Sarah's spirits up. If he had been all on her side and as enthusiastic about detection she would have flopped long since, but anger gave her energy. Adrenalin, she thought vaguely.

'It's time for me to meet the children from school,' she said. 'Make yourself comfortable, Vic, and try to think of something useful. Have some more coffee if you want to.' As she drove out of the parking place she saw his reflection in the driving mirror, through the wide window; he was getting himself a drink at the sideboard, and she hoped that Campari which was all she had would do him good. He seemed more overwhelmed now than he had done before they had returned to the Fosters' house in Orton to look up Mrs Knox's address. Actually it had never occurred to Sarah that there would be any difficulty about finding it, though her only visit there had been through unfamiliar streets some time ago, and she had not seriously expected that a visit to her would have any results. It just felt like doing something practical. It seemed so odd that if somebody was not in the telephone book there was no other way of finding out where she lived. The discovery of this re-

84

vealed to Sarah a great gulf in the system of civilisation.

Marcus and Emily were, as usual, about the last children out of school, and, as usual, came out scruffy and quarrelling. Sarah noticed with irritation that Emily had lost her hair slide again; and Marcus had a damp patch on the front of his trousers. She was embarrassed by them. It would have been nice to be able to present a pair of well behaved and handsome children to Victor, who would certainly have no sympathy or understanding for the toughness and tempers of normal ones.

As anticipated, both children groaned when warned that good manners were expected, even though Sarah had softened the blow with the promise of lollipops. Her method of upbringing was a combination of unrealised threats and bribes whose performance Marcus and Emily enforced.

Marcus had been sweetened slightly by the assurance that he would be able to inspect from the inside a really super car, and he set up a loud and babyish wail when Sarah swept into the turning and no visiting car was to be seen.

It appeared only too soon that Victor had hopped it. Nor had he left a note to say where he had gone. The only trace that he had been there was a dirty glass, and a mug which had tipped over on the goatskin carpet, depositing unremovable dregs. His narrow impression had already gone from the sofa. It made Sarah freshly aware of how insubstantial a person Victor was, light physically to symbolize his emotional elusiveness. When Jeffrey had reclined on that squashy sofa it bore his imprint for hours.

Sarah made some telephone calls; then she climbed on to a high stool and pulled down a small collection of emergency goodies – crisps, sweets and chocolate – and opened a couple of cans of cheap supermarket Cola. The children were running around the house quarrelling, as always after school. It had never helped her to be less infuriated by it to know that it was a manifestation of exhaustion due to hypoglycaemia, and that they couldn't help it until their blood sugar count had been increased. She shrieked at them now to come here at once, and perhaps some more than usual

85

conviction in her voice came through, for both Marcus and Emily appeared in the kitchen to see what she wanted.

'Look: tea,' she said.

The children shrieked and tried to fall upon it.

'No, wait a minute. Listen, Marcus, you're old enough to look after Emily, just this once. I won't take you to the school outing unless you're good; and there's the telly. I've got to go out for a little while.'

'You can't do that, Ma, it's against the law,' Marcus said.

'Only after dark and if there's an open fire,' she countered briskly and inaccurately. 'And you can jolly well make sure there isn't an accident.'

'Daddy will be furious,' the two children said in chorus. Sarah knew that Jeffrey would indeed be furious. Only the last Saturday she had said that Marcus might bicycle down to the shops if he stayed on the pavement and pushed the machine across the roads. But Jeffrey, who came home just afterwards, had leapt back into his car and roared off after his son; Marcus had later told Sarah, with a certain glee, that Daddy had been bonkers, and had chucked the bike into the car and chauffeured Marcus to the toy shop, tipping him handsomely into the bargain. But Jeffrey had been angry with Sarah for the rest of the day. If he came home to day to find Marcus and Emily alone in the house, for the first time, there was no doubt that he would be furious, but since it looked as though even greater causes for outrage against Sarah would be coming his way she would just have to risk it.

The children stood at the living-room window upstairs to wave goodbye, looking like waifs.

It took Sarah some time to find the address she had finally got from Marion Firth. On the one day she needed it, of course, the map of Orton was not in the glove compartment where it belonged, and she got lost on a maze of one-way streets which all seemed to peter out into residential cul-de-sacs. The whole Weston district was redolent of wealth and what Sarah chose to regard as philistinism. The houses displayed four-car garages, many of them fully occupied; and as she drove along peering at street and house names she heard the merry splashing of swimmers in heated pools, and the twang of tennis balls. An over-enthusiastic volley behind a hedge caused a tennis ball to slam against her car, and then roll back under it into the gutter. A scarlet-faced young man, dressed in white, ran out and called a cheerful apology after her. She stopped, and leaning out, asked him the way to Weston Grange Road.

'Turn right and right again,' he called. 'It's just over there, actually,' and he waved his racket towards his own privet hedge. 'Through those fruit trees, d'you see? Those are the back gardens in Weston Grange Road, backing on to ours. Are you house hunting? This is nicer, though I say it as shouldn't.'

'No, thanks so much. Just visiting.' In spite of her anxiety, and prejudice against business men Sarah found herself beaming at the young man. He looked so cheerful and unworried, like a hangover from the prewar London stage, she thought. She had never seen a play where an actor sprang through French windows calling 'Anyone for tennis?', but she suddenly realised that this catchword, a shorthand joke to her for everything that was reactionary and moribund in England, represented something as real as a kitchen sink. In Orton, matinee land was still going strong.

She drove even more slowly around the block, overcome by the thought that her whole errand was ludicrous. In these surroundings, how could she find a baby's abductor? It would not be startling to come in upon a wife-swopping party or even a teenagers' drug orgy. But an ordinary middle-aged woman, guarding a stolen baby, waiting for its ransom? As Vic had insisted, the whole thing was nonsense. But what else could she do but pursue this idea, the only one she had after all? She had already explained at length to Vic and persuaded herself again and again that telling the police was the last resort. It would be a comfort in a way to have reached that stage. But since it might even mean the end of her marriage, and probably result in the derangement of Flora Millington, she dared not take the step yet. The first result would be bad enough. She had been more and more aware as the day wore on how much she wanted to stay married to Jeffrey; boredom would never seem the same again, if she could ever achieve it. But to have Flora on her conscience would destroy her; she hadn't the strength. She muttered to herself, 'I'll just try this hunch. There must be a way out of this mess.'

Sarah was aware of schizophrenia in herself, as she crept on down the long road at two miles an hour. She knew quite well, intellectually, that it was impossible to suppose that her present quest could have any result other than acute embarrassment. At the same time, she had a background of a life in which nothing had gone wrong. There had been no tragedies, no disasters, no dramas even. And any apparent emergency was of a type which those tempered by life in the big world outside would regard as trivial – nothing which could not be mitigated or cured by telephoning a doctor, a funeral director, or 999. There were always competent professionals to take over. Nothing happened which would not, sooner or later, become a good dining-out story. So now, after thirty years of a life thus protected, she just was not able to believe that something genuinely dreadful could have happened to her. At the back of her panic-stricken mind, was the faint promise that everything would work out all right in the end, because it always did.

However, this comforting conviction was very deep buried in her consciousness when she reluctantly halted outside number 18 Weston Grange Road. It was a curious road to drive along, for it seemed deserted. One could have used it as the site for a film of suburbia after the extinction of the human race. The pavements were cracked, rough tarmac, with weeds growing on them; but the road surface was smooth and had been repaired, which just showed how the ratepayers got around. Sarah had some trouble finding the right house, for the numbers along the road were well hidden, though each house had its name proudly displayed. They were a fine collection of miniature stately homes; Sarah had noticed Chatsworth, Belvoir and Carisbrooke. Number 18 itself retained the name of the field on which it must have been built some forty years before. It was called Longacre, and the gate on which the name was embossed was firmly shut.

Standing on the pavement, Sarah looked up at the ugly house with indecision. Now she had got here, she didn't know what to do next. Could one march into someone's house and say 'Have you got my baby?'

All the windows were shut and closely net curtained. One could not see whether a car was in the garage, past the wooden screen which earlier in the day had defeated Mrs White, and the letter box in the front door was six inches from the ground. One could hardly peer through that.

Sarah thought, oh well, what harm can it do?, and gave a couple of hard pushes on the bell. She could hear it ringing, but no answering footsteps. There was total silence from within the house. She could not kid herself that she heard a baby crying. It was getting windy now, and she shivered, though not entirely from cold. The trees were swaying noisily in the breeze. There was a row of poplars which she could see running down the side of the garden, over the garage, and she thought at first that she was hearing the noise of running water in the house; but it was only the trees.

She walked to the side and tried to turn the handle of the door in front of the garage yard. It opened quite easily, and she peered around it, before stepping over the door sill into a small bare yard. Ahead of her was an empty garage. On her right was a high blank brick wall of the next door house; on the left the back door of Mrs Knox's house. She rapped on it loudly with her knuckles, and waited a couple of minutes. There were only two windows on this side of the house, a frosted glass one beside the solid door, and one above it, which was thickly draped, as the ones in front had been. Sarah rapped fruitlessly against the door again, and looked irresolutely up at the house, wondering what on earth to do next. She might just as well go home, since the house was obviously empty. But then, what? Ring the police? Explain to Jeffrey – who would by now be at home – why he had returned to find his children uncared for?

So far, she had done nothing which could not be explained away easily. 'Oh, I was just trying to visit Mrs Knox,' she would say. 'The front door bell didn't seem to work, so I thought I'd try at the side.' Dared she explore further? She felt as nervous as twenty years before, playing murder games in the dark in a strange house. She tiptoed to the back of the garage, and found a door which though warped and difficult to open, was not locked. She leant against it without result, and then kicked painfully out at it. The door opened at last, and she peered through it into the garden behind. It seemed far more like trespassing to go through to the back, and with a hazy notion of the law she wondered what penalties she might become liable to. Her nerve was on the point of giving way, and she walked irresolutely back through the garage when she heard a faint and plaintive wail. At first she took no notice, assuming it to be a cat; there had been a large and bushy one in the hedge while she stood ringing the front door bell. But when it came again she stood rivetted, straining her ears. It was a baby – a quite small, newish baby, crying somewhere near by.

At the same time as her determination renewed she was telling herself that there were bound to be babies in several of the houses round here. Hearing one did not prove anything. Yet she no longer thought of retreating; she walked through the back door of the garage into the garden.

It was a flat, square patch of land, uncompromisingly suburban there were neither the lush under and over growth of a country garden nor the basic lawn and surrounding oblong beds and paths of a town back yard. A well-cut lawn was dotted with flower beds, heart shaped or diamond pointed, displaying lobelias and geraniums surrounding weed free earth which was sparsely interspersed with matched roses. The noisy poplar trees were after all in the next door garden. This one was enclosed by an orange woven fence, which provided an ugly privacy.

The sound of the baby was louder now, and Sarah dared to think that it was coming from the house. All the windows on this side were closed, as they had been at the front, and even here, where no curious eye could possibly see, they were masked by net. She walked along the path beside the house, and pressed her nose against one of the windows but could see nothing inside the room. It would have been possible to do so upstairs for the slanting sun was still falling on the top half of the house, but there was no ladder, and not even a burglar-tempting drain pipe.

She tested all the windows, but none was unlocked, and she stood back baffled. Should she call the police now, on the strength of the baby crying upstairs? They would not believe that it was anything to do with her. Or get a neighbour? But they too would think she was a mad woman. How could she explain the fact that she had not called the police in the first place? Also it was almost certainly well known in the neighbourhood that Mrs Knox's public spirited profession was the fostering of orphan babies. They would never be persuaded to believe that there was anything suspicious about baby wails coming from her house.

Sarah stood back and looked up at the neighbouring houses. Behind the poplar trees stood a large red brick house with only one window that she could see facing in this direction; it had Micky Mouse patterned curtains drawn across, blowing in and out through the open window. Sarah was surprised to find that it was half past six already, past a small child's bed time. What on earth would Jeffrey be saying if he had happened to get home early? Thank goodness it was a Top of the Pops day; if he was, as usual, still working, at least the children would be safely telly watching.

On the other side the Knoxs' garden was overlooked by a slightly more modern house; just post war, Sarah would guess, with the windows recently replaced with plate glass. They were all Venetian blinded, which meant that Sarah could not tell whether anyone was watching her. At least it did not look as though anyone from the next door garden could spy through, for the fence on this side was reinforced by a privet hedge on the other. So she whispered to herself.

'Now for housebreaking, my girl', and turned to examine the accessible windows.

But it was easy enough to say; how on earth did one do it?

Once, several years ago, Sarah had been doing jury service at Quarter Sessions, and had been appalled at the apparent ease with which the accused men in the dock seemed to break into houses. The ones she voted guilty had at least been caught, though usually after disposing of their loot. But there must be thousands of others, she came home thinking, who made a comfortable living out of small domestic burglaries.

So she and Jeffrey had invited a crime prevention officer from the police to come and tell them how to make sure that it did not happen to them. It was a shattering discovery that short of having a burglar alarm wired direct to the local police station there was nothing much they could do. A determined thief, they were told, would not be deterred by any number of locked windows, though the casual one might be. Sarah had lived in the constant expectation of being burgled ever since. So now she reminded herself that if she was determined it should be possible for her to enter the house. The trouble was, what did the determined thief actually do, when confronted by rows of locked doors and windows?

She looked in despair at her hand, on which she had only a broad gold band on the fourth finger. The well-equipped house breaker would at least have a solitaire diamond with which to cut the window panes – though she was less depressed by this lack because she could hardly believe that a small diamond would really cut thick glass. She cast her mind back over stories read long since; didn't people use treacle and brown paper somehow? But it did not much matter that she hadn't any for she could not think what one should do with them.

Sarah took off her shoe, and hit it as hard as she could against one of the window panes. It made no impression at all.

Two other methods came into her mind as she stood pondering. One of the young criminals at quarter sessions had taken a ladder to the bedroom windows at the back of an empty house and climbed in upstairs. But not only did the upstairs windows here look as firmly locked as the downstairs ones, but there was also no available ladder. There had been various gardening tools in the garage, a motor mower, a rubber tined rake and a small ladies' sized fork and trowel, but she could not think of any way of making them work for her. Or she had read about sliding paper under a door and poking the key through on to it. She went back to the side of the house to inspect the back door again, and was foiled on finding that it was locked by a Yale. So she stood there helpless, without the faintest idea how to proceed; what was the normally educated and well brought up woman supposed to do in such circumstances? It was a pity, she thought, that the whole thing still felt to her dangerously like a game.

The baby was crying loudly now, she could imagine it arching its back and waving its useless arms in fury. It must have been left alone in the house. Why, she thought suddenly, I'd be performing a public service by going in to that child even if it is a perfectly legal foster baby. Nobody should leave a baby alone in the house – anything might happen. Suppose I hadn't come along, it might make itself quite ill. Margaret Knox must be a pretty peculiar woman in any case, kidnapper or no, if she has left the baby all alone.

Sarah went to knock and ring on the front door again; and when it was still unanswered she felt fortified by rectitude in her determination to investigate. She went to her car and lifted out the small plastic sack which had been kicked around unopened on the floor under the driving seat ever since she had owned it. There proved to be various incomprehensible tools within and she chose a stoutish metal bar. She went round to the back garden again, and after a furtive glance up at the neighbouring windows, swung it full strength against one of the small panes of glass in the leaded window. It shattered at once, noisily, and she jumped back appalled at herself, but there was no reaction from within or from either side, and she reached her hand in to the window catch, and lifted it upwards. The window would still not open, and she realised crossly that it must be further protected by a security lock. She was damned if she would give in; she had gone too far now to fetch help even if she wanted to.

All the windows here at the back were leaded downstairs, but the bedroom windows were sheets of glass. She went back to the garage again, and painfully and loudly dragged a small and a large galvanized dustbin back to the garden. It didn't seem to matter what noise she made, nobody was taking any notice. Just as well, she thought, that Orton was such an unfriendly place; would anybody take any action if they heard screams for help or shouts of murder? Quite likely not, she thought in disgust, and hoped that she would show more public spirit herself. She threw her tool up on the projecting roof of the bay window, and managed in the end to balance one dustbin upon the other – having emptied the smaller one into a flower bed first – and scrambled upon the infirm edifice. From that height she was able to see that the two neighbouring gardens were apparently empty; and the house behind in the next street was still screened even at this height by a prosperous looking orchard. Sarah pulled herself painfully up, hanging for a terrified moment as the dustbins fell away, before she managed to scramble upon the small platform. She found the iron bar at her feet, and attacked the window in front of her with vigour.

The noise sounded ear splitting to her as the glass broke, and she cowered facing outwards to see if furious citizens had at last been alerted; but then she was able to open the window by lifting the catch.

There was an inordinate amount of broken glass scattered on the window sill, roof and carpet, considering what a small hole she had actually made, and she cut her hand as she climbed in, but there was a box of paper handkerchiefs upon the tidy dressing table and she wrapped it up absent mindedly.

Sarah had climbed into a bedroom, and with only a quick glance around she went out of the room. All the doors on the landing were closed, but the baby guided her to its room and she went straight in. It was lying in a draped cradle, screaming and gasping and battering the air.

The baby was very small, bald and purple; it was wearing a frilled nightdress which Sarah did not recognise, and had been sick; there were dribbles of dried vomit on its cheek and on the broderie anglaise pillow.

Sarah looked at the baby, and felt as though her stomach was lying at her feet. It was a new born baby, which Cherry Millington was; like her it was hairless, toothless and pale. A hasty check of the disgusting nappy showed that it was a girl.

And Sarah just did not know whether it was the baby she was looking for or not.

XII

When the small grey van had driven out of the Knox's garage and turned briskly left into Weston Grange Road, Mrs White was not far behind. The only anxious moment was in that empty street, but it was natural enough to drive behind a neighbour's visitor along to the main road; and once they reached it, there was enough traffic for her to be satisfied that her own unremarkable car would not be observed trailing the van. She kept well in to the near side, because the van only had one wing mirror, and dodged dangerously along, with more of her attention on her quarry than on the other traffic.

Once out on the by pass it became easier still, and Mrs White followed a lorry or so behind the grey van, congratulating herself that she had filled up with petrol that morning.

The van was being driven by the same dark haired, uniformed woman whom she had seen earlier, and was easy to follow, for it went at a moderate speed and observed all the road signs. Really, the most difficult part came when she followed down the atrocious road which led into Lodworth. This was was a smallish industrial town, about fifteen miles to the west of Orton, and Mrs White had occasionally been there for furniture sales. It had a good grammar school, and some people who worked in Orton lived in the country between the two so as to be entitled to send their children to school in Lodworth. But the country was unattractive, and the town more so. The red brick back to backs were as insanitary as when they were built, and the shopping arcades and supermarkets, dominated by tower blocks which rendered the pedestrian walks so windy as to be almost unusable, were showing signs of degenerating into slums only half a dozen years after they were built.

Fortunately it was by now just before the rush hour proper began, and there was enough traffic for Mrs White's car not to be noticeable, and not so much that she was held up and lost track of the van. They drove through the middle of Lodworth, and the grey van stopped at every zebra crossing and amber traffic light; the uniformed arm made conscientious handsignals in addition to flashing the indicator. It was as though, Mrs White thought, the driver were determined not to be stopped by officious police on any conceivable grounds.

Mrs White wondered where they were going. The Mary and Martha Home could hardly be in Lodworth, which was still in the Orton telephone area, since it had not been traceable by her phone book researches. If they were merely visiting another client it might be awkward to make contact without embarrassment. On the other other hand, she would go mad if she were obliged to listen to squalling babies much longer.

Short as this digression from concentration had been, it had made her lose track, for a moment, of the vehicle ahead, and then, to her fury, she was stopped at red lights. She revved away from them as fast as she could, feeling sure that if the van had turned left or right at that cross roads, she would have noticed, and she drove too fast onwards, hoping to catch it up.

A long way ahead she saw a grey car turn left, and hoped it was the one she wanted. The difficulty was, however, that when she came to the top of the rise, there were three turn-ings to the left, very close together. She was in a district of slightly larger houses than the back-to-backs on the Orton side of town. Here were still red brick terraces, but looking more prosperous, and with tunnels through between each pair, presumably leading to back gardens. She turned into the first road on the left, and cruised slowly along it, until it came to an end at a canal, without seeing any car other than a couple of beaten up saloons parked at the side of the road. The second road was similar except that it made a loop by the water and came round into another, where there were houses on one side and a row of garages on the other. A lane ran down beside the garages, and Mrs White turned pessimistically down it. She was giving up hope, and won-dered how many days it would be before she saw the grey van again in Orton. She would simply stand in the road outside Mrs Knox's house next time and not let the van by until she had spoken to the driver.

The lane led through to an open space which looked like a bombed site, covered with rubble and rubbish, with more shabby garages round the side. There were some boys playing football who giggled at her, but their accents were such that she could not understand the obscene jokes which she felt sure they were making. She took a ten penny piece from her purse, and said,

'Did you see a grey van come in here?' One of the boys snatched at the coin and ran off with it, and another kicked his ball at her car; none of them answered, but before running away one pointed to the corner of the enclosure, and she drove slowly over the rutted ground in that direction.

XIII

Folly Armitage had come over from her Uncle's house to
attend the evening meeting in Vic's constituency, sitting at
the back of the hall and not drawing attention to herself.
She was wearing a plain linen dress, and had tied her hair
back under a scarf, but she did not really mind if Vic did
notice her before the end. She intended to make him take
her to dinner and show her the scenes of his youth afterwards. She did not know that Gordon Buddle was in the
hall as well, for he had taken good care that neither Vic
Nightingale nor Folly Armitage should see him. He had
hoped to be able to keep an eye on all Vic's local activities
today. He expected that something he did, or perhaps even
the sight of a more than usually doting fan, would give him
an idea for his next step. Gordon did not trust Folly
Armitage to find out all he needed to know, or to tell him if
she did.

It was infuriating to discover, when he arrived in the
constituency that afternoon, that Vic had sent a message to
say that he was delayed. Where could the bastard be? He'd
left London on time all right. They'd even had to cancel a
meeting of the Young Supporters Group because he hadn't
turned up. Quite a few of them had left the place Young
Antagonists, by the look of it. Vic had finally arrived at
five, just in time to forestall his Chairman's apologies at the
door of the party headquarters in Lodworth where he was
due to hold a 'surgery'; and then the queue had been kept
waiting for twenty minutes while he had what he called a
wash and brush up.

The party headquarters was in a dingy house on the
north west side of the little town. Vic had fought his
committee when they wanted to establish a branch there,
but they had insisted. None of their rivals provided any
facilities for constituents in the little town, and the com-

98

mittee had argued that the journey into Ferraby to see the Member was a great disincentive. They said it would be a vote winner to set up shop there too. In fact it was a back scratching exercise for the boys as usual, Vic had explained to Folly. One of the older committee members wanted to let off part of his house without the bind of having resident tenants. So he lived upstairs in this godforsaken red brick terrace and downstairs was a waiting room, a room for Vic, and a tiny shower and lavatory in what had been the lean to scullery, which jutted out into a back lane which Vic had described as full of rats both human and animal.

Vic was partly angry about it because the whole thing was a nuisance and a bore and he hated Lodworth even more than he hated everywhere else in the constituency. He also felt that such kowtowing was unnecessary. It was for himself that he was loved by the voters, not for any dreary attractions like surgeries. All he had to do was knock at their doors and kiss their babies and they voted for him in droves. He had always been fortunate in having the knack of inspiring devotion. This he had explained to Folly, who had passed it on to Gordon Buddle. He did not actually do anything to inspire the devotion, he had said. It was just something about himself. Not anything to be proud of or to be overmodest about. It was a physical trait, like blue eyes or a hare lip, just something one must accept.

It was painful for Gordon Buddle to be obliged to admit to himself that this was probably true. He would so much rather not believe it. But there was no doubt that they voted for Vic, and it was not as though he had earned their respect for his political achievements. A run of the mill back bencher, he was, once he got to Westminster. Of course the majority of Members were men; and women voters no doubt outnumbered the men here. It was the sort of charm which a middle aged woman would fall for, Buddle thought venomously. There had been a couple of them gazing at the poster outside the surgery; an unflattering photograph, Buddle thought, but the women were slack-jawed and gooey-eyed at the sight of it. The problem was where to begin with all the damned doting females who followed their Member around – how to single out the one who handed over the lolly. Not, he thought sourly scanning the audience, that any of them looked as though they had any.

Gordon was distressed to find that he was beginning intensely to dislike Victor Nightingale. He listened to the platitudes flowing over the enraptured audience and felt his face twisting in scorn. He hastily set it into impassivity again. Sitting unobtrusively behind a pillar in his macintosh and trilby, he did not want a personal expression to betray him; he hoped that everybody thought that he was a bored reporter. His shorthand was, actually, quite good, and he wrote down descriptions of some of the audience. But his mind was elsewhere. It was a nuisance if personal feelings were going to come into this. He liked to pride himself on being detached from his employers. Both they and the people for whom he obtained information about them should be nothing more than bread tickets to him. Old Champernowne had never registered as a person on his consciousness at all. The trouble was that he was jealous of Vic Nightingale. Not for his girl, naturally – Vic was welcome to that bitch – but for his ease in the world, his luck, his hypnotic appeal. Even without an additional subsidiser, it was a cushy job that Vic had. And he was no older than Gordon, no cleverer – hardly better educated, if you counted one public school as being the equivalent of a grammar school and redbrick: which Gordon did. Why should Vic have everything while Gordon just cleaned his shoes? It really wasn't right. It would give him a positive pleasure to provide that handle for our Mr Nightingale, Gordon decided. He'd enjoy thinking of him on the hook.

Gordon got up stealthily and tiptoed out of the stuffy hall; he had left his old car near by, and drove now towards the university.

Although Gordon himself had not been to one – perhaps because he had not – he was firmly of the belief that only Oxford and Cambridge were real universities, and he knew too little about the organization of such establishments to have any idea whether he would find anything open at that hour or not. He did not realize his unusual good fortune in finding the place illuminated and bustling. The campus was at the edge of the town, on as much of a hill as this part of the Midlands provided. There were four variegated tower blocks clustered around a former lunatic asylum with a fine disregard for any unity of architectural style. Separated from them by the town cemetery were the halls of residence; Buddle caught sight of some students playing the fashionable Ferraby game, a race round the graveyard without setting foot to ground.

Two of the tower blocks were in darkness, and from the site map at the entrance to the campus he saw that they were lecture and seminar blocks. But the Students' Union and the Central University Building were full of activity.

He strolled casually along. Nobody took any notice of him as he unobtrusively took his bearings. The two buildings were both in use for evening meetings of societies; in the largest lecture theatre the Professor of Environmental Studies was giving his Inaugural Lecture, as appeared from the posters and notices which Buddle read. He went into a bleak coffee bar in the Students' Union building. It was a huge room, brick floored, walled and roofed, with concrete pillars and stainless steel tables. It was as though it had been designed to withstand the assaults of any number of riotous inmates. There were various unriotous ones sitting around now, quiet and lugubrious couples nuzzling one another over their coffee and a few solitary students moping over piles of books. At one end of the room was a noisy group playing with a table football game; at the other a small and dirty counter at which to choose from unappetising snacks.

Nobody questioned Buddle's right to buy himself a cup of tea, and he took it over to a table where a young man who looked marginally livelier than the near corpses around him was throwing a set of dice right hand against left.

As he sat down Buddle laid his shorthand notebook on the table, and fixed what he hoped was a suitably brash and jaunty expression on his face.

'*Daily Echo*,' he said. 'Doing a background series on the

makers of tomorrow.'

'None of those round here.' The young man stopped throwing his dice and looked positively interested.

'Your alumnus of five years ago.'

'My what?' Buddle thought, I was right about these provincial places. He said patiently:

'An old student. Victor Nightingale, MP. I'm looking into his early life.'

'Yeah, I know who you mean. The only bright spark they ever turned out. There's a photo of him in the bogs. Don't know much about him myself.'

'Do you know anyone who might?'

'Try the porters. They know everything. Grass to the staff, too.'

'Thanks.' Buddle left the rust-coloured tea undrunk and set off. He found a uniformed porter behind a desk in the Lunatic Asylum. The hall was lined with marble and stags heads, with some examples of abstract art superimposed. The elderly man seemed out of place, with his row of campaign ribbons and air of independence, but he accepted a note from Gordon complacently. He was not reluctant to be reminded of Vic Nightingale; indeed, the reminiscences were produced with a fluency which suggested that those less interested than his present audience were frequently obliged to listen to them.

'A charming young gentleman,' it appeared that he had been, unlike most of his present-day successors. 'Always had a smile and a good-day, and not above the odd game of darts down at the local. Wonderful, how he was doing now.' It appeared that the old man followed Vic's progress in the newspapers with zealous loyalty. It was tempting to see him as Vic's financial supporter; but too improbable to be permissible. The man was obviously one of the old-fashioned 'good poor', with his suit pressed and darned, his health service teeth, and his pale, watering eyes. But he was full of information, and Gordon left him with a list of several students whom the porter remembered to have been good friends of Victor. None of the names meant anything to him, however, and it hardly seemed possible that someone

102

who had been a student only five years before should now be in a position lavishly to subsidise a contemporary.

Gordon's most useful haul from the interview was the address where Vic had lived during his three years as a student. He had never lived in a hall of residence at all, and according to the old man, this must indicate that he lived at home. The University was keen on keeping first-year students under its control, unless they knew that parents were doing so. The porter had eventually unearthed an alphabetic notebook from the recesses under his desk, with the addresses for letter forwarding. He was not supposed to keep these, he admitted to Gordon, but he never liked to throw anything away. It was a hangover from army days, when he had been taught that everything might eventually come in useful. Waste not, want not, he told Gordon rather severely. And, he added, look how useful it was now, he could find just the thing the gentleman wanted in a jiffy.

It was not too late to go to this address now; in fact it was a good moment, while Vic was tied up with his dinner. One did not want, after all, to run into Vic on the doorstep of his aged mother's house. And the old porter had given him very clear instructions on how to find Motcomb Street. He would never have managed it otherwise, for Ferraby was a maze of redbrick streets none of which appeared to be parallel, and several times Gordon found that he had driven round in a circle. However, once achieved, Motcomb Street proved to be as poor and dingy as he had guessed Vic's home background must be. He looked forward to telling Folly Armitage about it. But Vic's parents turned out to be dead, not merely disowned. There was a noisy family living in the little house, and over the blare of the television Gordon was told that the old Nightingales had passed on several years before. Not before time, he gathered, at least as far as the occupation of council houses went. This was a four bedroom one, and had been wasted on the old widow who had stayed on here for far too long after she was alone. No, the son never seemed to come home to see her. His photograph had still been on the walls when the Gardeners moved in. Mrs Gardener looked impatient as Buddle hovered on the step and shouted instructions about the chip-frying over her shoulder; she said she didn't know anything about the Nightingales' relations. There had been a cousin with a car who had cleared the last of the old woman's belongings out. No, Mrs Gardener didn't know her name. But she had come from over Orton way, that she could say. She'd left her address somewhere for forwarding any mail – not that there had been any.

'Mike!' Mrs Gardener shrieked suddenly, making Buddle jump nervously. A slouching man came out of the front room, shirt-sleeved and in braces. He glowered at Buddle and said to his wife,

' 'Aving trouble getting rid of 'im, are you? What's it this time? Brushes or encyclopaedias?'

'No, 'e wants that address. For sending things on for that Mrs Nightingale that lived 'ere. Somewhere over Orton.'

'I dunno where it is.'

'I'll send it to you,' she said, turning to Buddle, and beginning to close the door. He put his foot in the crack and said politely, 'I wouldn't want to bother you to do that. I'll come back in half an hour, you might have found it by then.'

He was pleased with himself as he returned to sit in his car. He listened to the ten o'clock news, thinking that old bag would never have sent him anything, she just wanted to be rid of him. But if she knew he would keep turning up, that might do the trick. He wondered whether to try to find the address of the Nightingales' relation from the council offices, but could not think of any plausible excuse for doing so, or of any way of ensuring that Vic would not find out that somebody had been asking questions. He hummed a tuneless version of 'The British Grenadiers', thinking about his bank account, and how much healthier it was than Nightingale's. But a middle-aged woman cousin with a big car might be just what he was looking for.

When he reappeared on Mrs Gardener's doorstep, she looked surprised to see him, but had taken his threat to reappear seriously, for she had an address written on a scrap of paper.

104

'In the back of the rent book, it was,' she said proudly. 'Knew I'd put it somewhere I wouldn't lose it.'

He read it as he sat back in the driving seat. Mrs Margaret Knox, 18 Weston Park Road, Orton, it read. Now why, he thought, did that ring a bell? Something he had seen or heard quite recently.

Buddle gunned his engine out of Ferraby, driving eagerly on what he was hoping would be a momentous journey. The first thing he'd been taught, in what he still thought of as his briefing sessions, was to distrust coincidence. Our Vic's going to come unstuck, but good, he muttered. Goody, goody, goody.

XIV

The news media had got on to the story very quickly. Mrs White couldn't quite think how, when she came finally out of the police station and turned on her car radio. The BBC seemed to hear things as soon as they happened these days.

Admittedly, she'd been stuck in Lodworth police headquarters for a ridiculously long time. They didn't seem to believe her. It was a great surprise to her to discover how long, hostile and elaborate the police dealings would be with a person like herself, a citizen of impeccable background and record, unimpeachably respectable and trustworthy. After all, as she said, she didn't have to tell them what she had found in that garage, she could perfectly well have driven straight home and left them to carry on as best they could. Such rubbish, expecting her to repeat and substantiate and detail her statement. Anyone would think that they actually suspected her of killing the poor woman herself.

Sylvia White was used to thinking of of herself as a weak and feeble woman, but was in fact as tough as they come, and this became apparent as she described her movements. Her timetable left no time for fainting or hesitation.

'You heard voices from the garage and listened?' the inspector asked again. 'Perhaps you would tell me again what happened?'

'Well, it was the only double garage, as I said. I waited outside for a moment. Then I was just going to give up the whole thing when I heard sounds inside. A door opening at the back, and a woman's voice. It said "What on earth are you doing ..." and then she started to whisper and I couldn't make out any more. There was a man talking too, I could only hear odd words. He was telling her how badly he needed something, and I think she said something about not deserving it. They were at the other end of the garage, I really couldn't hear much, but I thought I'd wait till the woman came out, because I did want to speak to her, as I told you. Then I heard the man's voice say "I can't risk it", and there was a gasp and a thud and the door at the other end slammed. And that was all I heard.'

'What did you do then?'

'Oh, goodness, you've got it all down in triplicate already.'

The Inspector glanced across the desk at her. He had a tired face, long and drooping, with thin black hair draped in strands across a sharp domed head. His suit was shiny and creased and he had a row of pens in the breast pocket. Sylvia White thought, in a spurt of spite, that it was monstrous that a man who looked like an inefficient clerk should have so much power over her. He said:

'Please tell me again what you did next.'

'Oh, very well. I knocked on the door, and there was no answer. Then I saw the little boy I'd spoken to earlier, standing behind me. He must have been watching me.'

'He says that he went home to fetch some sweets, and he didn't see you at all at the time when you say you were listening outside the garage door.'

'Oh well, there he was, anyway. So he said he'd open the door for me the way he often had before. Not that I could understand most of what he said, atrocious accent they learn nowadays in these schools. He climbed up the brick side of the block of garages and ran along the parapet at the top, most dangerous and unsuitable place for small children to play, their mothers ought to take better care of them, and then he dropped through the skylight and let me in through the garage door. It had a Yale lock on it. So I gave him some money and went in.'

'Yes, go on.'

'Must I go through all this again? I don't like to remember – however. There were two cars in the garage, a Morris Traveller and the grey van I followed from Orton. There was some furniture, quite inappropriate and peculiar, a dressing table, piled with cosmetics, one of those folding plastic wardrobes apparently full of clothes, a suitcase, some scattered paper on the floor. But you know all that. I bent down to look at the paper on the floor – it seemed to be typed and duplicated messages, with blank spaces left – when I noticed a dark, gooey puddle spreading towards me from under the car. I thought it was only petrol, but it looked rather disgusting and I jumped back. Then I edged around to have a look on the other side of the car. And you know what I saw.'

'Tell me again.'

'It was a woman lying on the ground. For a minute I almost thought she had two mouths, parallel, yawning open. Disgusting. I turned away at once, naturally, but not before noticing that the front of her suit was saturated with blood. It was the uniform of the Mary and Martha Maternity Home. And the little van had its name on the side. But the woman was Mrs Knox, I was certain of that.'

'You were expecting to see Mrs Knox?'

'No, I told you, I was expecting to see the woman driver from the Maternity Home.'

'I believe that Sergeant Harvey has told you that no such establishment appears to exist.'

'How should I have known that?'

'Have you any explanation for the fact that the driver of the van and your neighbour seem to have been one and the same person?'

'I find it hard to believe ... even with a wig, one would have thought ... Still, it's all a total mystery to me.' She pulled on her pigskin gloves, one fraction of her mind admiring their smallness and cleanliness, as she listened to the policeman ruffing through the pile of papers before him. Everything in triplicate already, she thought half contemptuously, half afraid.

Inspector Young folded the pink file on his desk and rubbed both his eyes with rough forefingers. He said, yawning,

'You might as well get on home, Mrs White. You'll not be going away anywhere for the time being, will you? One of the officers will run you back to your car.'

'The only thing is, the baby,' she said. She didn't give a damn whether anyone looked after the baby or not, she thought, but she didn't see why she need ever endure the sound of its crying again. 'If there is a baby at Mrs Knox's house, hadn't a policewoman better fetch it? There may not be anyone to look after after it.'

He looked at her as though she were mad for a moment, and returned his weary eyes to the papers. 'That's all right, madam, all taken care of,' he said, his voice failing at the end of the well worn formula. He opened the door of his small room for her to go through, and a reflex of femininity made her flash her eyes up at him with a smile of thanks as she passed. He was yawning, mouth uncovered, and eyes closed. It was, after all, nearly the middle of the night.

Her own house was heavenly quiet to come home to. She had never so much welcomed its air of order and tranquillity. What bliss to make oneself a warm drink and sit dressing-gowned in a pink and private bedroom. She hardly ever thought of Jack; he was only too easy to put out of mind. But now she glanced at her single bed with love, and looked at the unmarked, pale carpet and starched organdie valances with adoration. Jack had only to enter a room to have it in disorder. He would have trodden on the frills and torn them nightly, sat on the bed, emptied his pipe into the crystal bowl in which she deposited her jewellery, and abandoned his clothes – dirty and even smelly – on the floor where he stepped out of them. And she had always known that it was her duty to clear up after him and endure his

108

masculinity till death did them part. How fortunate it was, she thought, that one's son could live five thousand miles away without the admission that they could not bear to be together.

There was no crying from the next door house. At one moment she thought she heard the tinkling of broken glass, but nothing else. Only the poplars tossing in the wind, and the pathetic complaint of her housebound puss; imprisoned for her own good, she thought fondly. It would be such a disaster to have any underbred babies. She would find an aristocratic husband for the darling, she decided. Now that her peace and quiet would return, there would be plenty of time for thinking about that sort of thing. She had been neglecting her poor pets recently, but they should have it all made up to them.

Sylvia White read a couple of pages of the thoughts of Patience Strong. Then, not unlike a cat herself, she stretched herself out in the pink satin sheets and switched off the rose shaded light. Her last thought before sleep was of gratitude for deliverance.

XIV

Jeffrey arrived home at the same time as Sarah, and he was so abstracted, as often, that the children's eager sneaking did not register on him, so Sarah escaped any reprimand for having left them alone. It seemed, she thought, to have been a great success, for they had even cleared up their own tea, and went to bed like lambs once she had dealt with the miserable baby.

Emily displayed a brassy indifference to the child, and Sarah recognized her own attitude in her daughter's, but Marcus seemed quite interested in the only form of dependent life which had so far been allowed in his home. He did remark that he thought a kitten, or even a gerbil, would have been better still; but he wielded the tin of powder and the nappy pins with voluntary attentiveness.

Marcus's mother would normally have welcomed this behaviour, and watched him with sentimental pleasure; but this evening she wished him anywhere else. She was torn between the wish to finish this chore and get down to the next ones, so that the two older children would be in bed and Jeffrey's supper eaten and cleared up before midnight; and the need to examine the child in minute and concentrated detail, in the hope of recognizing unequivocally some feature on her body; the superficial likeness to the remembered Cherry, might so easily, so calamatously, be spurious. And, oh Lord, what then?

How Sarah regretted the impersonality of her earlier dealings with Flora's baby. If only she had admired and exclaimed with the eye for detail which, she told herself bitterly, any normal mother would have given. Why had she never compared the baby's features with its parents', or laid the tiny hands beside Flora's to see how alike they were? Her glances had been polite and brief, and her congratulations and compliments as meaningless as if she were a walking talking greetings card from the shop down the road. She racked her memory, as Marcus chattered, for the sound of Flora's voice. Had she not heard Flora remark on some mark on the baby's body, or comment in exact terms on the shape of nose, or the length of the lines on her palm? Sarah herself had an amateur interest in palmistry and had scanned her babies' life lines almost as soon as they were laid in her arms; but she had never been sufficiently interested in Cherry Millington to do so for her.

But Sarah's memory was almost exclusively photographic. She could not recreate the sound of Flora's words in her head. She looked at the child with a picture in her mind of herself doing so that morning as she changed nappies and aimed the teat at an eager mouth. But that morning her attention had been concentrated on the immediate future. She remembered now, as she sat again plugging the baby's mouth with a bottle, how she had forced herself to patience so that Cherry would be satisfied and sleep. She had not seen these soft cheeks and screwed

110

up eyes then; between her and them had intervened the clothes from which she might choose, and the picture of Vic, overcome with pleasure at the sight of her, as she had been sure he would be, in a motorway cafe.

Cherry Millington was, she remembered having noticed, a nondescript baby, the sort that came by the thousand. She had not wanted to claim ownership. She recalled how she had felt a faint and self-satisfied scorn for a baby which was hairless, round and sallow of skin. Marcus and Emily had entered the world dark-haired, with porcelain complexions; Sarah had occupied her idle hours in making partings on Marcus's tiny skull, and round bubbly curls on Emily's. She remembered the alertness of their new-born expressions, the certainty she had possessed that they saw and knew her. She had been educated to scepticism by the time the second one was born, but when she saw her had known that this child at least could see and hear. There was no reason, she had thought, why her own children should not be prodigies. Time and habit, and the developing bloody-mindedness of children, had taught her better. She was under no illusion now that her children were prodigious in any way, except perhaps, tiresomeness. But at least she knew them when she saw them.

Jeffrey came into the spare bedroom as she sat gazing helplessly at the gorged and sleeping baby. He looked at it with a sentimental expression, and said:

'Sweet, isn't she? But what about supper? Or is Cherry making you feel broody, old girl?'

Sarah dumbly shook her head. She felt as though she were trapped in a cage made of a tiny fine nylon mesh. If she pushed hard enough it would give, but outside was a quagmire.

'When's Flora coming for her?'

'She's staying in hospital till tomorrow.'

'Oh, you mean the baby's staying?' Indulgence changed quickly to dismay, when Jeffrey realized that sleepless nights and late meals would be returning to his house. Babies were all very well in theory . . .

Sarah thought, I'll go mad waiting. Suppose Flora comes

111

home and it's not Cherry? She'll know at once. It might so easily not be Cherry. It was a crazy idea to go to that house at all. And yet, it must be, it looks like her. I'm just being neurotic. Of course it's Cherry. I've just got a thing about it, like wondering whether I've turned the gas off. I've always turned it off, when I get home. What other baby could this be? I did see Margaret Knox in that car park, after all. I'll go back tomorrow and see whether there's a marked nappy in the bucket. I should have looked. I could have found out whether the clothes Cherry was wearing were in the house – I'd have known them. What if Margaret came back and it wasn't Cherry and she's called the police? They'd trace me easily. Maybe I'll go back tonight.

Eventually, after displaying such tightly controlled calm as to make the children suppose she was ill, and behave worse accordingly, and after setting everything that Jeffrey could possibly want to eat before him on the table, Sarah said that she had gut trouble and retired to the bathroom. It was the only place where she could be alone; and even then, Marcus came banging on the door with a rare determination to wash his hands.

She sat huddled on the bath mat with her face in her hands, elbows on her knees. Thoughts surfaced slowly and meaninglessly over in her mind, like dopy porpoises.

She could give in now and tell the police; it would entail confessing that she had broken and entered Margaret Knox's house, and Flora would receive the shock from which Sarah had been anxious all day to protect her. And of course, Sarah would herself come in for immeasurable blame, for her original carelessness and for not getting the police at the moment she discovered the baby was gone.

Or she could hang on to the baby she had. She said inanely, 'One in the hand is worth two in the bush', and Jeffrey called up to know what she had said. None of the rooms in this flimsy house were soundproof. And then Flora would come home and be handed the infant. It might be all right. That would be the greatest relief that Sarah would ever have experienced. But suppose it wasn't? That did not bear thinking about.

Or she could go back to Margaret Knox's house and try to find something which she recognized as Cherry's. This seemed the only thing which she could see herself doing.

Sarah got up and looked wearily in the mirror. There were black smudges of mascara below her eyes and the rouge, applied aeons ago that morning, stood out now in clownish blobs on her pale cheeks. She dabbed some vaseline on her dry lips, and went down to explain to an oblivious Jeffrey that she had a date to visit Margaret. She added a good deal of circumstantial embroidery, but he was absorbed in a pamphlet and only grunted.

It was raining, and the yellow street lamps reflected shining shadows on to the road. The light dazzled through her dirty windscreen and Sarah drove more by guess than vision. But she found her way to Weston Grange Road, and parked, with more caution than she had shown that afternoon, around the corner. She walked along the slippery pavement regretting her mission but realising its inevitability. The corporation was saving money here, presumably because any ratepayer in this street would have his own headlamps to show him home, and of the widely spaced street lamps only one in three was lit. Sarah started nervously as a cat ran in front of her, and she kept her eyes fixed on the ground as she answered a dog walker's greeting. She had started to turn in at the gate of number eighteen before she realised that there were several cars parked in the road just there; the house was lighted and the front door open. She stopped short, and was about to go away as quickly as possible, but her arm was gripped by a man who had been invisible in the shadow of the fence. She screamed, but was calmed by the sight of his warrant card. The policeman seemed to take her terror for horror; for no suspicion appeared as a result of her claiming to be just visiting, and any hesitations in her story could be attributed to shock at the news of her friend's death. And though the fear of personal involvement played a large part in the shock, it was certainly true that she felt the hot and cold all-over quivering which the news on its own would have induced. Death had never come her way before; and even less accompanied by policemen and the guilty knowledge of having, that same afternoon, broken into the victim's house. For it appeared early on in her conversation with the constable at the gate that this was a case of murder. They were making no secret of it.

The news was splashed all over the next day's local paper, having only rated a tiny middle page paragraph in the *Guardian*. Sarah, clutching the putative changeling on her lap, read it with incredulity.

The headline was 'Local Woman Murdered', and her provenance seemed to matter more than the manner of her death. Margaret Knox's husband was indubitably abroad at the time, which left no obvious suspect. At the time of death he had been attending a trade fair in Wrotslav. Her throat had been cut, and the reporter was delighted to report that the garage in which her body had been found had been swimming in blood. Why she should have been in a garage at Lodworth at all remained undisclosed, and the reporter was obliged to curb his dramatic instincts with the final sentence that the case was being treated as one of homicide.

Local rumour filled out the picture pretty quickly, and it did not take long for Sylvia White's story to get circulating in Orton. And as soon as she heard of the clothes and wigs in the garage, and of the two cars in it, it became crystal clear to Sarah that her suspicions of Margaret Knox had been justified; and that the child on her lap was indeed the one which had been stolen from her. She looked at the sleeping face with a dawning affection, and the remembered picture of the infant she had seen in Flora's arms, and the one present before her now, merged in her mind into one. Of course this was Cherry; and what a fool she had been to doubt it.

But her problems were not so easily solved. Though she could at least face calmly the prospect of Flora's return from hospital – this afternoon, thank God – she was now forced to agonize over what to tell the police. There could be no doubt that it would help them if they knew what she did. They might then be able to search among the parents who had suffered from Mrs Knox's profession. It seemed only too likely that another bereaved parent had discovered her identity and exacted revenge. On the other hand, it would be so easy to say nothing about it. Vic would presumably now disappear from her life, and once Flora had collected Cherry she could go back to being a provincial housewife. The whole episode could be regarded like a perverse period of banging her head against a wall; so nice to stop.

Sarah like to think that public conscience would have won this internal battle. It was, in the event, resolved by the appearance of last night's plain clothed policeman at the front door, who identified himself by showing his warrant card; he was Detective Sgt Smith.

Sarah found that she could not manage to tell a coherent story which was only half the truth. Within half an hour she had told him everything she knew, though she managed to get by with just saying that 'a friend' had been with her at the time of, and after the kidnapping. She admitted that the friend was a man, who lived in London, but the policeman seemed prepared not to be told his name.

He said suddenly, 'Can you prove that you weren't in Lodworth at all yesterday afternoon? And what time did your friend leave you?'

'It was about four. But of course I wasn't in Lodworth. Oh my God. I know what you're getting at. You can't seriously think that I – do I look like a woman who could cut someone's throat?' She realized as soon as she had said it that it wasn't a very sensible remark. The normal badinage which she might enjoy with a youngish man didn't dent the severe features of this Puritan.

He said, 'You have razor blades in the house, I suppose.'

'No, we both use electric razors.' And that was another remark she would have preferred not to have made. She felt unkempt, and her stomach was playing up again. But he'd interpret it as a guilty conscience if she went to the bathroom, especially as he'd be able to hear if she were sick, or anything else. She willed Cherry to start crying.

The young man walked over to the sideboard, still not

115

properly cleared from the last three meals. Jeffrey's construction was on a tray between the fruit bowl – two mouldy grapefruit – and the porridge saucepan. It was a model in detail, such as architects show clients, of a hospital, to be built, by a complicated process of local political chicanery, on a sports field. A new sports field was then to be put on a plot of waste land belonging to one of the two councillors. But Jeffrey had a mind above such sordid details, and he was eating and breathing this hospital, for the time being. Sarah told him that his stooges should do the models, but he liked fiddling with cardboard, glue and balsa wood and said it gave him inspiration. It was just one more thing that this house was really too small for.

'Are you doing this?' he said.

'No, it's my husband. He's an architect.'

'How does he do it? The cardboard and wood come in great chunks, don't they?'

'Yes, there's a knife there. One of those triangular blades screwed into a thick handle – a lino cutter, you know? It'll be on the tray, we try to keep it away from the children, they're terribly dangerous – oh!' she clapped her hand over her mouth in a classic gesture, and stared at him as he looked along the sideboard. 'You don't think that I – ? It was there yesterday, I saw it there.'

'I believe you,' he said. 'But where is it now, Mrs Foster?' She went and stood beside him, looking blankly at the sideboard. It was messy, certainly, but one could see at a glance that the lino cutter wasn't there.

'Well.' The policeman moved towards the stairs, 'You won't be going anywhere, will you Mrs Foster, except locally? We'll be getting in touch with you again.' He was half way down the stairs, Sarah meekly following him, when he added, 'You've got a solicitor, have you? It's not my place to suggest it, but you might perhaps be advised to get in touch with him. Good day.'

The baby started crying as Sarah shut the door, but she was sure there was something more urgent to do than deal with her. Ring Jeffrey? Ring a solicitor? She didn't even know any, here, though one could probably look it up in the

116

yellow pages. She didn't know what to do but felt harassed and hurried all the same. But her digestion was the most urgent. Her guts felt as though they had turned to water. Emotion always gave her diarrhoea, but combined with this permanent feeling of queasiness it really made her feel quite ill. She crouched on that lavatory and sobbed in self-pity. How had a perfectly normal little adventure turned into this nightmare? Other women managed to meet boy-friends for coffee without the skies falling in on them. What have I done to deserve all this, she thought?

It was time to feed that blasted baby again, and then she must buy some food. If only she didn't feel so awful. Where was that knife of Jeffrey's anyway? Surely he had been using it last night. But an effort of thought recalled to her a picture of Jeffrey reading last night when she went out, as she had said, to visit Margaret Knox. Well, one of the children must have borrowed it when they were alone in the house. After all, she knew perfectly well herself that she had not driven to Lodworth and killed Margaret Knox. It would be difficult to prove it, but Sarah didn't even know where Lodworth was, though it must be somewhere near Ferraby, since she had heard Vic moaning about his surgery there.

Just as yesterday, when she had had to force herself to believe that Cherry Millington had really become involved in crime, and it wasn't all some mad treasure hunt, now Sarah could not register that she was concerned in an official murder inquiry. It was too far removed from her experience of life. She took the baby down to the playroom on her shoulder after absent-mindedly feeding it, and looked in the battlefield-like mess for the lino cutter. The door had been shut on the chaos for too many days, and the floor was carpeted with pieces of toys, some of them glued together by red paint which had spilt out of a tin which one of the children had 'borrowed' from the garage. The smell made Sarah feel sicker and she went upstairs again and propped Cherry on the sofa – with some difficulty because the leather was so slippery – and made

117

herself a hot milk drink. If ever nerves needed soothing, hers did.

So unreal was Sarah's attitude towards her present position, that she actually found herself thinking that in order to get rid of Cherry for an hour or so she might ring up Margaret Knox and ask whether she would take over. Sarah was at this point of mental disintegration when the doorbell rang again, and she found two men, this time, with a police car behind them.

She was shown two more warrant cards, and said rather helplessly, 'But I've just told one of you everything I know.'

'Who was that, madam?' said the man in plain clothes. The uniformed man behind him took out a notebook and a pencil.

'It was Detective Sergeant Smith. I saw him last night, outside Mrs Knox's house. He's only just left.'

'I'll use your telephone, if I may.' The man went in and spoke in a low voice presumably to his headquarters. Then he said, 'We haven't any record of your seeing one of our men last night.'

'But why are you here then?'

'Are you the owner of car number UBC 426C?'

'Yes, but do you mean to say that this is just for parking or something?'

'I'd be grateful if you would come to the police-station, madam, and let us have your finger prints and a statement.'

Sarah was obediently getting her coat, when her brain cleared, and she remembered not only the baby, who could not be left alone upstairs, but also an article in the last week's colour supplement.

'Are you arresting me?' she said.

'No,' he answered, looking resigned.

'Because I'll make a statement – though I think it's inefficient to make me do it again – but I'll do it here.'

'Very well.' The man sat down, and the other one went and sat in a corner with his pencil at the ready.

'How did you get on to me, if it wasn't that chap I saw?'

118

'I may as well tell you, madam, that a car with the number of yours was seen parked outside 18 Weston Park Road during the late afternoon of yesterday. There are also fragments of black jersey, such as the lady driving it was said by our informant to be wearing, caught in the upstairs window at the back of the house.'

'Well, I'm not denying it,' she said crossly. Her fingerprints, she thought, must be all over the place. No point in denying even if she wanted to. So she made her statement all over again. This time the policemen seemed quite uninterested in the identity of her companion in the motorway cafe, accepting it as natural that she should have met someone there for coffee, and that 'my friend' should then have tried to help in the emergency. The telephone rang, during her recital and was answered by the policeman. He sounded puzzled, and asked Sarah to describe Detective Sergeant Smith. She concluded that he must have been from a rival police station or something. But it didn't seem very interesting.

Sarah felt like death by the time these two finally left, saying they would be back, and nearly cried when the bell rang yet again. But it was only Flora eager to collect her baby.

Flora came up the stairs with Sarah and went ahead into the bedroom. Sarah waited for a moment outside the door, wondering whether in spite of all her new certainty, Flora would scream and faint and deny that this was her own daughter. But that at least Sarah was spared. Flora picked up the child with manifest joy, and looked dotingly at the tiny face before kissing it all over. She said:

'I couldn't bear it without her. Even twenty-four hours, you've no idea how awful it was.'

'No, I like it if my two are away,' said Sarah drily. She did not offer coffee, but Flora followed her downstairs and sat rocking maternally on Jeffrey's bentwood chair.

'It was lucky I did get back today, because I only just remembered about your trip to Grande Hall. That's tomorrow, isn't it?'

'Oh – I'd forgotten all about it.'

'Gosh – I'm surprised that Marcus and Emily let you. I thought they were thinking about nothing else. It should be rather fun.'

'I don't know that I can face it.' Sarah had two swift and conflicting visions; one of driving thirty miles each way with the children quarrelling in the back and the other of refusing to go after all and the children giving her hell at home. 'I suppose I'll have to,' she said.

'You did promise them, that they could go at half term. They were longing for it, I know. As a matter of fact, I'm looking forward to taking Cherry to places like that. It will be such fun too see her reactions. I suppose she's too young to enjoy it, really.'

'Yes, much.' Sarah had a moment of affection for the child, simply because she was the right one. 'Here, let me have a hold of her,' she said, but Cherry was instantly sick on Sarah's shoulder and the emotion quickly passed. 'I'll get her things,' she said.

'Yes, I suppose I'd better go home. George is away, you know.'

'Well, I have to go out, actually.'

'Oh,' said Flora a little blankly. But she gathered up the carrycot and suitcase, and Sarah helped her across to her own house. They could hear Sarah's telephone start to ring as Flora stood fumbling for her key, and Sarah dashed back shouting goodbye over her shoulder. It would be Jeffrey, she thought, wanting to know what the hell was going on. If only she had decided what to say to him.

But all he said on the telephone was that he was coming straight home, and would pick the children up from school on his way. Sarah was pleased to wait in until he came. In an uncharacteristically meek voice she replied, 'Yes, Jeffrey' and went numbly upstairs to make a placatingly proper tea. The bread was still unbuttered when the doorbell rang again.

Victor looked as suave and soigné as though he were straight from a gentlemanly barber; as usual, his face looked as though he had never had to shave it, and his suit was sharply pressed. The handkerchief in his pocket matched the subdued tie, and Sarah could see her face in his shoes. Gazing at her with his intensely blue eyes, and smiling his politician's smile, he asked whether he might come in for a moment.

'Oh, no, Vic, not now, Jeffrey will be home any moment. It really isn't a good moment. I don't think you'd better.'

'I just wanted to ask you what had happened about that baby.'

'No thanks to you, everything about her is all right,' Sarah said with a minor resurgence of spirit. 'What happened to you yesterday anyway?'

'I waited for a while until I thought you had forgotten me. And then I thought I'd better get on to the constituency. I was pretty late at the surgery as it was, after all, I didn't leave here till half past four.'

'Before that, Vic. I was back here myself by ten past.'

'I think you're mistaken,' he said, fixing her again with his blue gaze. 'Half past on your clock. And that tallied with my time of arrival in Lodworth. After all, darling, you're not the world's best time-keeper.' It gave Sarah a peculiarly disagreeable sensation to hear Victor use an endearment to her, partly because it was on Jeffrey's doorstep, and partly because, apart from that painted smile, the impression Vic gave her was of purpose and almost enmity; certainly not of love. His hand was in his pocket, and from the bulge she thought it was clenched. She said quickly,

'It's five past now. Do go, Vic, the children will be here with Jeffrey any minute. They always get home at this time, just as we did yesterday. I know you're wrong, because Playschool was just starting on the telly when I went out again, and that's at twenty past. One lives to a telly timetable with small children. But it doesn't matter, actually I noticed last night that the sitting-room clock was wrong, so I suppose you felt as though you'd waited longer for me. Anyway, to make a short story out of it, I broke and entered Margaret Knox's house, Cherry was there and her mother collected her today. And I may have to tell the police that I spent the day with you. I'll try not to. But it may not be possible to keep your name out of it.'

'I can hear your telephone ringing, do go and answer it,' he said.

'I can't hear it.' She turned to listen, and shook her head. 'You've got division bells on the brain.'

'Won't you invite me in for a moment?'

'No, Vic. Not with Jeffrey coming home. Please, please do go. You can't want to meet him.'

'But I want to talk to you.'

'Have we anything left to say to each other?' Sarah felt repelled by the impersonality of his gaze, it was as though he saw her as a substance to be moulded to his will. Well, he wasn't mesmerizing his voters now. Sarah felt herself to be immunized against Vic.

'Meet me for lunch tomorrow, OK?' he said, in a voice which would have ravished Sarah a week ago. She still saw its charm, but she was beginning to feel sick again, and without make-up and knowing that she had not combed her hair, it was easy not to respond.

'I can't tomorrow, Vic, really,' she said. 'I've got to take the children to a school fete at Grande Hall. Ring me up, later on. In a few days, maybe. Now, do go, please.' She started to close the door, and he turned away. She could see his silhouette through the reeded glass as he stood hesitating outside, but eventually he walked away, none too soon, as Jeffrey arrived with the children just a moment later.

Marcus and Emily displayed at its most infuriating their uncanny instinct for knowing when their parents wanted to talk uninterrupted by children. Although it was their favourite television programme that day they hung around in the living-room, and neither cunning suggestions nor outright commands would budge them. Sarah had turned on the set in the playroom, and the music could be heard from downstairs, but at any given moment until eight o'clock one of the two children was in earshot. Jeffrey and Sarah spent the intervening four hours making polite conversation like strangers, larded with the explanations the children demanded of every sentence and with furious blandishments to them.

The fine edge had worn off Jeffrey's anger by the time he

felt able to question Sarah, and he said quite mildly:

'It's a bit much, you know, to have policemen coming to the office with crazy stories about kidnaps and murders and not to have the faintest idea what they were talking about. What is all this anyway?'

'I'm sorry, darling. Only yesterday was such a dreadful day I just couldn't talk to anyone about it. And then with Cherry crying so much in the night – there really wasn't a chance this morning. And I'm really not feeling too good at the moment either. Must have eaten something.'

'OK, OK, that seems rather too many excuses.' Sarah glanced, startled at her husband; that was not a remark that she would ever have thought to hear from him, since he was normally uncritical and receptive in a passive sort of way which had often annoyed her. So she hastily told him the same edited version of the day before's events which she had told the policemen; and the third time of telling it almost felt as though it were true. All she was doing after all, was excising one fact; that of Victor Nightingale's existence. She ended up meekly,

'I thought you might be quite proud of me. Breaking and entering, I mean, after all, you always think I'm so wet.'

'Mmmm.' He looked at her without a particularly proud or affectionate expression on his face, and Sarah again felt that this was not quite her normal Jeffrey. 'That's the true story, is it, Sarah?'

'Yes, of course it is,' she said indignantly. 'My God, you don't suspect me of driving to Lodworth and cutting Margaret Knox's throat, do you?'

'No, I'm sure you wouldn't be capable of it. Oh well.' He sighed, sharply, and went on as though he had an invisible agenda. 'And what about my lino cutter? It wasn't there last night, you know.'

'Well, Jeffrey, for goodness sake. You know how those blasted kids are always taking things like Sellotape and scissors. I expect it's in the playroom. D'you want to go and ask them?'

'No, I dare say you're right. But it's a bit awkward, that policeman noticing it wasn't here today. She must have been killed with a weapon very like that. When we find it, I'll get rid of it, by the way. Don't like the idea of having it around, with the children, now. And then, not only is our cutter missing, but you admit that you broke into the murdered woman's house, and you can't prove you didn't go to Lodworth yesterday. You can see why they're wondering about you.'

'But you don't?'

'Not about that, anyway,' he replied forbiddingly, and sat brooding as Sarah got heavily up to clear the table. It had been a scrap meal, and Sarah felt even less well than before. Jeffrey said suddenly, 'Did I know her, actually? I can't put a face to the name.'

'I don't think you ever met her. I do try to protect you from my boring acquaintances. I think we might have seen her once, when we took the children for a Sunday walk. You were cross with them, because you thought they were talking to a stranger.'

'That woman. Yes, I do remember vaguely. Did you see a lot of her?'

'Quite a lot, in a masochist sort of way, if you know what I mean, darling. It wasn't that I liked her so much, but she dropped in from time to time, and used to meet me for coffee. I think she was lonely too. I mean —' Sarah went on trying to smooth over tactlessness, since she wanted Jeffrey in a good temper – 'Well, it's not all that much fun for me here you know. I do miss our friends. Anna, and people.'

Jeffrey did not comment, and Sarah realised that she had complained of her exile rather frequently to him. Maybe he did hear what she said even when he never answered. He said,

'What were you doing half way down the motorway in the first place? Shouldn't you have stayed at home if you were looking after Flora's baby?'

'I never offered to do it. She just landed the baby on me without notice. And I'd have taken Emily or Marcus in their carrycots. How could I know that there was a madwoman parked beside me?'

124

'And why were you there?' he persisted.

'I was going to view a sale, darling, in Buckinghamshire. Pictures and antiques.'

'Yes, well.' He got up dismissively and said that he was going out. And she was so cowed that she did not even ask where.

XVI

Gordon Buddle decided that he had been as clever as clever. His brain had been working in top gear the whole day, and when he heard the news on his car radio of the horrible Lodworth murder he quick-wittedly turned his car round and landed just where he needed to be. The coincidence that he had been on his way to see Margaret Knox at the time was odd; but he could pride himself on the way his brain had invented a suitable plan for the new situation.

He had to admit that he had been helped by the fact that one of his school contemporaries had gone into the police force. The little camera provided by Handles Ltd. had come in very useful at the last old school dinner, and reproducing the warrant card of Detective Sergeant Smith of Cannon Row Police Station had been childishly simple. Whether it would stand up to proper examination was another matter. But since he, Gordon, had the foresight to ring up Lodworth Central Police Station on his way to the town, he was accepted without a word of argument.

'This is Inspector Gordon, on loan to Cannon Row, London,' he had said in a brisk, no time to waste voice. 'Just to inform you that one of our men is following up a homicide which took place here in London. Seems to be taking him your way – hope that's all right. Be glad if you'd let him have all facilities.'

He seemed to have gauged the formula closely enough for the man at Lodworth to be unsuspicious. This was something which happened several times a day, he knew from the real Detective Sergeant Smith. So he added for good measure 'Be grateful if you'd let Orton and Ferraby know, if you would.'

'Detective Sergeant Smith' had duly turned up on the job, waved his warrant card at the local bods and joined morosely in. He had decided that an air of sulky boredom would be the safest to assume, grunting when spoken to and repelling idle chatter.

It was as well that he had decided to be a non-speaker. The least opening of his mouth might have stopped him swallowing down the sickness which the smell and sight of all that blood in the garage at Lodworth produced. It would be an awful give-away for a supposedly hardened professional. And the sight of the body was almost too much for him: that dreadful gaping bite out of the neck, the bleached look of the skin, like the brains which Gordon sometimes cooked after prolonged soaking, the clothes matted with blood.

He turned his back with an assumption of blaséness, and while he listened to the remarks of the men behind him looked at the furniture which was set against the walls.

The dressing table was a whitewood one with triple mirrors, and there was a stool in front of it. The black wig had been put down beside a wig stand, and there were various cosmetics on the table, which he did not recognize. But it was plain that there were more colours of make up than one woman would normally wear, for he saw lying side by side tubes of light and dark foundation cream. There were also a couple of sticks of theatrical greasepaint, and a tub of cold cream. The woman lying on the floor had been in stockinged feet; on the floor were two pairs of shoes, one of brown suede shoes with a small heel, the other sensible black lace-ups which looked as though they were meant to go with the uniform the woman was still wearing. In each of these was a small pad which would fit under the heel. As he looked at them, a voice behind him said, 'Oh, cheek pads too, I see,' and a finger pointed at two pieces of foam rubber on the table which Buddle had not himself recognized.

126

'I'm Kirby,' the voice said, friendly enough. 'Glad to have you with us. Neat collection of disguises, isn't it?' Buddle grunted, and moved over to look at the clothes hanging in the plastic container. He listened to the conversation continuing behind him.

'She must have changed her appearance completely with all this,' Kirby remarked. 'Wig, built up shoes, cheek pads. Her best friends wouldn't have known her.'

Through the closed doors of the garage the noise of a crowd of people was increasing. Buddle decided that he would have to wait until he could leave under cover of the other policemen. The last thing he wanted was to be questioned by reporters.

'What about her home, sir?' a polite voice asked, and Kirby replied, 'Oh, the Orton police have started over there. Inspector Young will be going over when he's finished with the woman who found all this.'

'How did the BBC get on to it so quickly?'

'That damned boy. Must have told his dad, I suppose. Still, we'd better go and tell them there'll be no statement tonight. Clear a way for the mortuary van, too.'

Buddle followed as Kirby and the younger man went towards the door. The crowd surged forward as they saw the slit of light widening between the garage doors, and Buddle muttered what he thought would sound natural enough to the younger man, 'Tell him I'll report to Inspector Young, will you?' and edged his way unnoticed away around the edge of the crowd. He looked back when he reached the entrance to that piece of waste ground. It was almost dark by this time and the huge policeman was framed in the strip of light behind him. On the roof of the garages a uniformed constable was standing, presumably so that nobody could spy through the sky light; and as he went past the end of the alley which led along the back of the garages, through which the murderer must have entered, Buddle saw another pacing up and down.

He drove fast from Lodworth to Orton, but got lost in the surburban streets, and by the time he found Weston

127

Grange Road there were several cars parked and the house was lit up at all windows.

The dead woman's address had not been given out on the news, and there were no sightseers standing around. Gordon Buddle wondered whether he could work the same trick twice. There might be some useful information to be picked up in there. On the other hand, if Kirby had passed on some suspicions to Inspector Young, they might be waiting to pick him up in there.

As he stood in the shadow of the gate, his macintosh collar turned up against the relentless rain and his trilby hat pulled well down, he heard the hesitating click of a woman walking slowly towards him. He turned into the drive and he stepped forward holding his warrant card in the light of the street lamp. He was thankful for the rain; if there was a policeman on guard, he must be round in the shelter of the doorway.

And of course, his gamble came off magnificently. It was with the most fervent self-congratulation that he drove off, five minutes later, to his commercial travellers' hotel. There was this woman, thinking she'd given her name and address to the police, ready to make the most detailed of statements. Just waiting, she'd be, to tell him all tomorrow morning. He'd wait till the husband was safely out of the way. But the marvellous thing was that when he'd heard her name, he knew that he was nearly there. Our Vic connected up with Margaret Knox; his constituency office was two streets away from that garage; and now, here was Vic's bit of fun, snooping around at Mrs Knox's house. Useful knowledge, just waiting to fall into his hand. Gordon Buddle slept like a log.

XVII

The schools in Orton seemed to have an inordinate number of holidays and half days, and one acquaintance of Sarah's was making pocket money from running a dumping centre for the school children of working mothers. Sarah dithered the next morning about making use of her. But apart from the fact that she was usually booked up weeks ahead, Sarah was uncomfortably aware that she had promised to take the children to the fete at Grande Hall. From what they said, the whole of Orton would be there. The idea of the long drive, while she was still unaccountably feeling so unwell, was depressing; but at least she would spend the day out of the reach of policemen and others. In fact Marcus and Emily were relatively good on the congested way to Grande, and concentration on the road took Sarah's mind off her symptoms. It was a misty but dry day, and the summer countryside was agreeably green and flowered. Marcus made false and adult comments about how beautiful it was; he caught a bored grown-up's intonation precisely, enthusing about the unsprayed hedgerows and the buttercup-sprinkled fields. Jeffrey's parents had come down to Orton the Sunday before and taken the children for a drive after lunch, and their predictable reactions were reproduced by their grandson.

Grande turned out to be one of those places that make a driver feel that 'they' keep moving it further away; it had said thirty miles from Orton on the brochure, but Sarah was sure she had driven more like fifty when at last the AA signs started pointing towards it. She was already dreading the return journey, by which time the children would be peevish and fractious and have nothing to look forward to to keep them good. There were hundreds of cars, waiting to enter the drive, which was flanked by a pair of pillared lodges. The drive had been embellished by a whimsical hand, and dwarfs, gnomes and plaster squirrels could be glimpsed among the oaks. They looked like the products of a modern gnome factory, and one could only suppose that the tradition of oddity was handed down in the owner's family. For there was a miniature railway which had been a conceit of the previous owner, installed for his private convenience and gratification. The brochure explained how shooting parties had been conveyed to the butts from the house on it; and how, during the war, it had been used to concoct deceptive photographs for propoganda purposes, along with the miniature fleet on the lake. The Victorians, it seemed, had provided no such ornaments for their property; but a Regency incumbent had dotted the park with follies. For anyone in a good mood, it would be a delightful place.

Sarah made a conscientious effort to be cheerful, as her children squeaked and squealed at each new glory. Their enthusiasm was not damped even by the sight of the queue waiting to get into the train. It stretched half way round the perimeter of the car park and it took two ice lollies' licking time for those at the back to get to the front.

Sarah felt as though she had never been a child. Surrounded by jollity, enthusiasm and optimism, she was as sunk in depression as though she were at a funeral. The sun came out, and she tied her own and the children's jerseys around their respective waists. She was sweating, and wiped her forehead repeatedly with the back of her arm. Her eyes aimed as low as her spirits, she gazed gloomily at the ground; it was trodden dirt, bordered here by nettles, strewn with empty crisp packets and lolly wrappings. The air smelt of petrol and people.

The others in the queue bore waiting more cheerfully, chatting and behaving as though this was a welcome holiday. There were women in low cut patterned dresses and men wearing short-sleeved shirts hanging outside their trousers, and innumerable children. Sarah, in paint-stained jeans and one of Jeffrey's vests, felt almost ashamed for not being dressed in different clothes. In certain places, she thought, she would have been type-cast herself, but not here. However, what might have been a perverse self-satisfaction at being so utterly shabby in public turned to embarrassment, when she heard a familiar voice beside her.

It was Victor again, and, knowing what a sight she must present to his smart eyes, Sarah was far from pleased to see him, or rather, that he should see her. The children did her little credit either, she thought, as they played in the dust, being matey with all the others around them.

'What a peculiar place to meet you,' she said spitefully.

'Yes, isn't it?' he replied, and waited placidly beside her as the sluggish line of people moved forward; if he had come to meet her specially, he had timed it well, for by the time he slipped into the queue beside her Sarah was nearly at the front of it. There was a ticket office in the paint and pomp of the old Great Western Railway, and a chocolate and cream coloured train, its carriages open and two-seated and about four feet long, waited behind a puffing steam engine. A properly uniformed driver and stoker waited on the little platform, one of them shovelling, the other rubbing unnecessarily at a shining brass bell. A guard stood watch and flag in hand, and, since it was that sort of day, stopped the flow on to the platform just before Sarah and her party reached it. 'Next train in ten minutes' he said, and with pre-war sounding whistles and chunters the locomotive moved forward.

Marcus and Emily were enraptured at the sight, for they only knew of the existence of diesels; and, as Emily said in a shamingly loud voice, she didn't think she had ever been on a train. Sarah could only hope that she would not go on to remark, though it would be true, that she had never been on a bus either. One would deserve to be lynched by the surrounding proletariat if she did.

Victor did not explain his presence, nor, when she glanced at him, did he look out of place. His shirt, admittedly, was tucked inside grey trousers, and he had rolled the sleeves up; but he had not labelled himself with a scarf in the open neck, and in his dark glasses he looked convincingly like an Orton father giving the kids a day out. At least, nobody seemed to have given him any undue attention. Which was just as well. Even Marcus and Emily seemed to take his arrival for granted, and when Sarah said, 'This is Victor, children,' Marcus merely answered, 'Yes, I've seen him before.' He had not, but it was not worth arguing about.

There was room for two grown-ups in each little carriage, and the children went in the next one, behind their mother, along with a couple of Indian children. The train made a surprising noise once it started moving along; it felt as though it were going fast as the trees flashed by, and the illusion was preserved by miniature telegraph poles and bridges. Victor leant forward, now that nobody else could hear, and said

'I really wanted a chance to talk to you. You weren't very welcoming yesterday.'

'I didn't feel it.'

'Because of the family, you mean?'

'Partly. But you hadn't shown yourself exactly a knight in armour the day before.'

'My image is more up to date.' He leant forward to put his hand on hers, but the train drew in at that moment to another tiny station, where there were several platforms and even a turntable, with a spare engine on it. The two other locomotives worked a shuttle service, apparently, for as their train arrived the other moved off back to the car park, all its cheerful passengers waving and exclaiming.

Sarah found that they had arrived beside a lake, where a miniature ocean liner waited to take the passengers on a scenic tour of two islands, a heronry, and a model yacht harbour.

'I must talk to you,' Victor muttered, as they jostled in the queue to board the liner. Emily and Marcus were stepping on to the gang plank as Vic came level, behind them, with a naval uniformed man who was punching the tickets.

'Good morning,' Vic said. He handed over a note. 'Will you take these children on the bridge with you? We'll wait on the shore.' Wails of bereavement forestalled by the prospect of such glory, Marcus and Emily followed another sailor up three wrought-iron stairs to a well fitted out boat

132

deck. Reluctantly Sarah followed Victor as he pushed back through the crowd again, and they stood waving as the brave craft pulled away. Smoke poured out of the striped funnels and ropes were coiled as though there were the Atlantic ahead. The children, just the right size for the small-scale life belts which dotted the rail, waved with wild enthusiasm, and as the ship got further out in its sea, Marcus could be seen tugging on the spoked wheel, with indulgent help from the captain. The name on the ship's stern read 'SS *Queen Victoria*'.

'Was that necessary?' Sarah enquired coldly. 'Your King Cophetua tricks don't impress me.'

'Well, I wanted a chance to talk to you. Come and have some tea. The liner takes at least half an hour to go round.'

'How come you're so at home here? Have you been here before? I shouldn't have thought that amusement parks were in your line.'

'Only my line if they're profitable. This one's on its last legs, I doubt if they'll keep it going another year. Running costs too high. You get far more profit out of fruit machines than miniature railways. I doubt if even this bean feast will help much.'

'How on earth do you know?'

'It belongs to Folly's uncle, I thought you knew. I was coming down for the weekend anyway, and they didn't mind my making it a day early for the fete.'

They were seated by then, in a tea garden, so full that Vic had again been obliged to produce money in order to get a table. They sat on wrought-iron chairs, right by the water of the lake, and the tea, when it came, was China with lemon, and in a porcelain pot. Each table had a striped umbrella shading it, and on a bandstand which must have come from a municipal park a dejected-looking band was playing. The noise was extreme, and under its cover Vic and Sarah were safe from being overheard.

'Why do you want to talk to me anyway?' Sarah asked. 'I'd have thought I was superfluous with Folly around.'

'You could never be that.' He gazed at her with his warm

133

hand on hers. 'There's something between us which has nothing to do with marriage, and other people, and everyday life. Don't you feel that? As though, in some other life, we had been so close that nothing could part us now. Being friends with you is so important to me, you know, Sarah. One can have a lover any time, anywhere. But there aren't many true friends around. One or two in a lifetime, maybe. I feel as though we could never let each other down.'

Vic's deep, smooth voice was like a benediction. The patterns of leafy shadow changed on her legs and where the water reflected their movement. It was almost like being hypnotised, she felt so sleepy. Vic's caressing voice murmured on, about the importance and permanence of their relationship. They were to be loving friends, he proposed, and she nodded in soporofic agreement. He went on to talk about the episode of Cherry's kidnapping, and how distressed he had been for her.

'Waiting there, in your house, I was consumed with anxiety for you,' he said. 'It felt as though someone unutterably precious to me was being sucked into a world of ugliness and horror from which I couldn't protect her. You were gone such a long time.'

'Not really' she said lazily. 'Not long, just time to get to the school and back.'

He leant intimately close, and spoke with his mouth against her cheek. 'Half an hour at least, more in fact. It was five o'clock before I got to Lodworth. I heard your clock striking the half hour before I left.'

'If you say so,' she muttered. It wasn't worth arguing about.

'Sarah?' He held her chin in his fingers and turned her face to his. He would have done better to leave well alone, but he gazed into her eyes again, and said insistently, 'So you know it now, don't you, my sweet? You could swear that I was in your house at half past four?'

Sarah's internal photograph album flipped open at the picture of Victor as she had seen him that afternoon, when she left to fetch the children from school. He had been standing at the sideboard, she had seen him through the

134

picture window in the driving mirror, and she had hoped that alcohol would do him good. He had been picking up – her thoughts paused as words would have done if she had been voicing them. She had seen him pick up the bottle, she thought, to pour himself a drink. But there had been something else on the sideboard, she could have sworn to it. Something which was missing now; something which Victor could have taken.

She thought nervously, this man is sensitive. And she got up quickly so that he would suppose the sudden rigidity of her muscles had been preparatory to movement. She said lightly,

'Vic, did you know Margaret Knox?'

He put some money on the table and took her elbow. They walked towards the pier. The *Queen Victoria* was in sight coming round the second island. He said, 'Who?'

She thought, he's stalling.

'The woman who kidnapped Cherry' she said. 'She was murdered on Wednesday. Did you know her?' He did not answer straight away. Then he said, his voice low and controlled, wooing her still,

'I did, yes. Terribly tragic thing to happen. She was a distant cousin of mine, as a matter of fact. No secret about it. Her husband will tell the police if I don't. But there's no point in my making much of that. I hadn't seen her for years. I've lost touch with my family, in fact. You know how one does. We never had much in common. I prefer to have friends – like you, Sarah.'

'But you knew her well as a child?'

'She was years older than I was. Fifteen, at least. She rather worshipped me, to tell you the truth.' His voice became indulgent and reminiscent. He could play it like an instrument. 'You know how it is, a rather plain older girl with a baby cousin who's sweet and clever – she used to look after me a lot. Thought nothing was too good for me. Poor thing, she thought I'd end up Prime Minister, no limits to her ambition at all. When I went to the university, that was the beginning of my great career, she was certain of it. She'd have backed me to beat the younger Pitt, except that she didn't know any history. Poor old Madge.'

'So you saw a lot of her?'

'At one time I did. But it's a long time ago now. She used to tip me when I was a spotty schoolboy.' Victor looked at Sarah with a candid and rueful expression on his smooth face. 'I don't suppose I was kind enough to her, boys are such brutes. I should have realized how much it meant to her. But it's all long ago now. Water under the bridge.'

'Victor: do you remember the first time I met you?'

'Yes,' he said instantly. 'At the Garrowby's Hogmanay Party.'

'No, Vic. I didn't mean that. The second time if you like. It was in that damned cafe on the motorway. I was going to London and I sat down at your table because Margaret Knox was there. You seemed to be complete strangers. I introduced you, remember? What was all that about?'

'So you remember that, do you?' he asked thoughtfully. 'I'd almost forgotten. But that was the only time you saw us together.'

'What about all this famous truth between friends then?' snapped Sarah. 'On Wednesday, when I met you there, she had just been with you, hadn't she? You made her leave before I got there. Why did you meet her like that, all those secret assignations in public places? Were you ashamed of knowing her? Wasn't she grand enough for you? And what about the babies? Were you in on that? Were you, Vic?'

'No, no, I promise you, darling, not that.'

'If you weren't, then what were you doing, meeting her in hole-and-corner secrecy, pretending not to know her? What had you to do with her?' Sarah forced from her own mind the memory of Vic's arm seen through glass, reaching towards her sideboard. It was something not to brood on, a mad, nonsensical idea, like when one had an impulse to leap up in the expectant hush of the theatre's great moments and start singing.

'Just being friendly, Sarah, nothing else. Like meeting you, in the same places.' He added, after a pause, 'I didn't

136

tell you, darling, so that you wouldn't be jealous.' And with those words Sarah surrendered her disbelief. It was so ludicrous, so utterly absurd, that Victor should suppose, or say that he supposed, that she, Sarah, might have been actually jealous of Margaret Knox of all people, that it must be true.

The compulsion to believe that everything was normal in the most ordinary of possible worlds was such that Sarah hooked her arm in Vic's with a comfortable feeling of a friend won for life if a lover lost, and she waited amicably beside him for the return of the *Queen Victoria*.

They stood on the dockside, watching the manoeuvres of the liner as it edged in; the job was as complicated, apparently, as if the ship were life-size. Sarah could see her children tugging at the captain's sleeve, oblivious of her. She wondered whether this experience would outweigh the memory of the icecream cone on the way home, which was normally the only detail of a treat that seemed to make a lasting impression on them. The children joined her on the platform, radiant; Victor was still with her and Marcus thanked him spontaneously for buying the VIP treatment. As they were pressing into the train, with the same anxiety to sit together as if they were going on a jumbo jet, a tall blonde girl came to stand beside them. She was un-made-up, and wore white, filthy jeans and a transparent shirt. It took Sarah a moment to recognize her without make-up; it was Folly Armitage.

'I couldn't think where you were, Vic darling. I've been playing Red Indians with all the children,' she added, smiling at Sarah. 'War dances and wigwams – the lot. And they were teaching me about woodcraft. Cutting blazes on the trees, and all that.'

The engine started to hiss loudly, and they moved off.

'I did enjoy it,' Folly shouted, as the train gathered speed. It was going even faster than on the outward journey with an almost frightening momentum. 'Have you ever done it? Look, I'll show you.' She took something out of her pocket and started to carve an F on the wooden seat. Sarah leaned forward to see, but as she fixed her eyes in-

137

credulously on Folly's knife. Vic's hand shot out towards it. 'What"s that?' he demanded harshly. 'Give it to me! Folly jerked her hand back, and laughed.

'D'you want it?' she jeered, 'Buddle gave it to me. Catch!' She threw the razor knife in his direction, but several feet in the air. Victor, whose back was to the engine, stood up to reach it. He could not see that the train was approaching a bridge at speed.

Victor's head thudded against the arch of the bridge. They could hear it against the rattle of the train. He fell inert on to Sarah's lap.

XVIII

The Grande Hall arrangements for wounded visitors were as smooth as everything else Sarah had seen there, and Victor was carried away, with herself and Folly in attendance before much of the visiting crowd could have noticed that there was anything wrong. Sarah's children were left in the charge of the engine driver; they would not miss her for hours, she thought gloomily, as she waited in a small sitting-room. It seemed that the big house was no longer lived in; Folly and Victor had come for the weekend to one of the lodges at the drive entrance which was kept for her uncle's guests. He lived in the other lodge, presumably in equal discomfort, and spent six days a week at the local British Legion club to avoid those who provided his income. The surrounding estates, built in conformity with council standards, were far superior to the little house where they had taken Victor. This was a damp and ugly late Victorian cottage, with one room downstairs into which the front door opened and presumably a couple of bedrooms above. The chairs were landlady moquette and there was a very old copy of *The Field* lying on the pitch-pine mantelpiece.

Sarah looked restlessly out of the window again. Would it be dreadfully heartless and improper to leave without

138

hearing how Victor was? Anyway, it wouldn't much matter if Folly did think something scornful; just as it didn't matter if the children behaved atrociously where nobody knew who they were. She had the same mixed feelings which she had overcome the evening that she climbed into Margaret Knox's house; there was someone upstairs whom she wanted out of her life as soon as possible, and escape was the obvious answer to that. And also there was Victor upstairs, who had tried – there was no getting away from it – to con her into swearing that he was in Orton at a time when he might well have been in Lodworth, killing, for it was no use skating around that idea anymore, killing a woman who turned out to be his cousin; Victor, who had been panic-stricken at the sight of a lino-cutter knife, and who had had an opportunity of stealing Jeffrey's. He must have wanted to put the knife back, yesterday when he pretended to hear the telephone. One could walk out of the life of an ex-lover, but a cold-blooded murderer might not let one escape.

In a desperate attempt at rationalization Sarah tried to work out what was best to be done. Her main aim, in all this mess, was to keep it a secret from Jeffrey. What a blessing normal life was, she thought sanctimoniously. No more discontent at the kitchen sink for Sarah Foster.

She came for the third time to the picture of Lady Marcella Belvoir holding the spaniel which she closely resembled, and let the magazine slide on to the floor. The noise of children in the playground came into the cottage. The merry-go-round sounded like a barrel-organ. Folly had disappeared saying she hated sick people, three-quarters of an hour before. The doctor had still not come. Sarah peered out through the leaded windows. Nobody in sight, but freedom only the length of the drive away. If she retrieved the children and just went home, nothing could happen to her. Folly Armitage would think she was rude, and so what. Sarah turned the handle on the front door and stepped out into the sunshine. She was feeling rather sick again, and thought she might have some marquee tea with the children before the drive home; on second thoughts, perhaps a tearoom in the nearest place would be better. She would have to think about what happened at Grande, but later would do. The first thing was to get well away.

A voice behind her said, 'He's asking for you, Miss.' It was a matronly woman who looked as though she belonged here, but she was putting on her hat, pinning it with a firm jab. 'Can't stay, sorry, Miss. I told Felicity so. One till four, that's my hours, now I got to get back for my family's meal. Stayed late as it is, and that's what I will not do. In the bedroom on the right, Miss, go straight up.'

Sarah looked at her retreating back in despair. Why did people never behave the way they should? A woman like that ought to thrive on taking care of a young, handsome, wounded man, she ought to be bustling around with hot bricks and drinks. Instead, there she was walking squarely up the road, shaking other peoples' business off her feet. 'I could do that', Sarah thought. 'Just go, and leave Vic'. But her feet took her up the steep stairs, and she went in to the room where Vic was lying, contriving somehow to look interestingly pale, but wide awake. Why couldn't he have been concussed and unconscious for weeks? But the man who carried Vic here had explained that the bridges were made of rubber bricks, painted to simulate stone. Just in case people didn't take any notice of the warnings to stay seated, the insurance company had insisted. Not tough enough to kill a man, they weren't.

Victor flashed his eyes at Sarah, and said, 'Come and sit down, darling. I'm not dying. Poor girl, were you worried?'

'Not in the least,' she said, but he made his face sympathetic all the same, pursing up his lips in a soundless tut-tut.

'What were we talking about?' he said, watching her. 'I've forgotten.'

She moved out of his reach. 'You were persuading me that you had been in my house at the time when your cousin's throat was cut.' She thought as she spoke how rash she was, and backed quickly to the door. He said, 'Stop' and she turned half round to look at him. He was sitting on the edge of the bed, unruffled, his turquoise eyes glistening in a pale face. In this hand was an aerosol can, pointed at her face. He said softly,

'This is one of the perks of my job. It's an American patent thief catcher which we're going to have to stop by quick legislation. Very neat, it only blinds and scars. Though no doubt anyone who sprayed it in her own face would blunder through an open window like this one to the gravel below. What a tragedy, with me helpless in my bed, having begged you not to fiddle with the contents of my pockets while you came sick visiting. It does seem a shame, a pretty face like yours.'

XIX

Sylvia White rather enjoyed the knowledge that people were pointing her out and whispering about her at the fete. There were gratifyingly many people who seemed to know who she was, she must have had more customers than she knew. It gave her quite a feeling of being a romantic hero- ine, wronged and persecuted but soon to be vindicated. After all she knew quite well herself that she had not killed Margaret Knox. Soon enough no doubt the police would realize it too. Not that one minded being followed around all day by a handsome young man. It might even be rather a thrill, to one who was safe in the conviction of innocence, if he suddenly produced a warrant to arrest her, and swept her off before a silent, gaping crowd, in a Black Maria.

The 'tail', she believed he was called, had not made much effort to conceal himself. And it was with a feeling of conscious gaiety and gallantry that she decided to let him know that she knew he was there. She had a picture of herself as persecuted, injured, and brave. In any case, her purchases were too heavy to carry all the way to the car park, and there was a huge queue for the little train. It had been partly the knowledge that people were watching her that made her buy so much, but the jumble and antique stalls had been full of what she really liked to buy. Mrs White prided herself on forestalling trends, on buying cheaply this year what she would sell for a handsome profit next year. So her arms were full of things like beaten copper trays depicting the Taj Mahal, and a crinolined telephone doll, and a set of genuine pre-war flying ducks for the living room wall.

She stumped off towards the drive, resisting the temptation to nod and smile around like royalty, and once under the shade of the trees, turned around to the young man who was making a half-hearted gesture towards concealing himself behind a tree.

'Come along out,' she said. 'I know you've been following me all day. You can make yourself useful, carry some parcels for me. I wouldn't like to see my son Sebastian let a lady wear herself out when he could be of use.'

They walked side by side after that, but the man was too shy to talk, and obviously felt that he had failed in his duty in some way. But Sylvia White's spirits, already high, soared at the thought of how jealous her supercilious young assistant would be to see her escort; she hummed a tune and tripped merrily along on her unsuitably high heels.

Without this day-long euphoria she probably would not have had the nerve to enter the little house. It was partly bravado, wanting to show the young policeman how far from guilty and worried she was, and partly the fact that just after she caught sight of a truly irresistible umbrella stand through the open door of the cottage, she saw the back of a young woman whom she knew disappearing up the stairs. Another Orton customer, she was sure. So when nobody came, in answer to her tap on the door, she said,

'Do come in with me, I simply must have a wee look at this adorable place. It's probably full of lovely things, and the owners may be longing to sell them. Oh, look, what a wonderful case of stuffed birds – and do look at that fish. That must have been a proud catch.' She edged into the living-room, and glanced professionally around. The young policeman was clearly much embarrassed. Then she caught

142

sight of a corner cabinet standing on the turn of the stairs. 'I must just have a wee peep,' she said softly. 'Don't be so shy, my dear boy, what can happen to you? You're like my son, he always looks as though he's ashamed of me. But it's not even housebreaking, the door was wide open.' All the same, she tiptoed quietly up the stairs. There were voices coming from the bedroom at the head of them. The first few words meant nothing to her, but then she stood spellbound, gesturing her detective to be quiet. He looked as though he longed to interfere, if only to get himself out of an awkward position; but his orders must have been merely to follow and report, and he stood uneasily below her on the stairs, his arms full of parcels, and listened also, perforce, to every word.

The woman's voice whispered, 'But you can't mean it. You're not – you're teasing me.'

'I wish I were. I'm not a violent man, I hate the idea of blood and thunder. But I have to protect myself, surely you see that?'

'Yes, but I don't see, I don't understand. Why did you —?'

'I never meant to do it. I don't like hurting people. I don't want to hurt you. It's something I daren't risk though. That's what I told Margaret. I didn't want to have to do it, she made me. I only wanted to make sure, I thought I'd frighten her into going on if she had really been so crass as to change her mind. But I'm sure that she felt the same as always, deep down. She adored me you know, I was the only important thing in her life. Nothing else mattered. Everything she did was for me, she lived and ate and breathed for me. That's why she wouldn't have minded the way she went in the end. That was for me too, like all her life.'

'But why —?'

'I needed the money, of course. She always sent me money. I couldn't live on the meagre screw I get paid. I mean, you've seen how I live. It would have been a bed-sitter in Clapham and a cheap hotel in Ferraby, on that. You can't wonder that I spent all she sent me. She knew I needed it. Though she thought it was all going in the fund, of course.'

'The fund?'

'The party fund.' His voice was impatient, didactic. 'The collection for the new party. We were to take over the country. I was to be the saviour, get us out of this mess we're in. I could do it, too.' He paused, seeing himself as the second Messiah. He must have looked like that, visionary and noble, to Margaret. 'Don't you see, we'll never get out of the mess we're in until one strong man comes forward as leader. Somebody young, with vision and ability, someone whom the others will follow without opposition. It's only a matter of biding one's time; there will be the right moment, I'll recognise it. And then, all problems will be solved.'

'Are you the strong man?'

'Of course. So you see, Margaret had to work for me. It wasn't just sentimentality, not mere family affection. There's a great future ahead, and she lived and died for it.'

'What was the money for?'

'Oh well, all political movements need money. Can't do anything without money these days. That's why I'm not there yet.' His voice was brooding and angry. 'Never enough money. Oh, I suppose she did her best. She thought there were other contributors too, of course. But what was I to live on? I needed what she sent me for everyday life. She was naive to suppose that one could build up party funds from that. I had to spend it. Don't move, Sarah,' he said loudly, his voice suddenly sharper. Outside the door, Sylvia White was frozen to attention, like the terrified woman inside it. The policeman had abandoned his passive role. He stood on the step, beside and pressed against Mrs White, making gestures at her to tiptoe away. He scribbled a note saying, 'Go and dial 999, say PC Banting and where we are,' but she refused to move without his protection and stood trembling, but listening. She feared that if she went down the stairs, that door would open and a fusillade of bullets be fired at her. The man inside, whoever he was, seemed to be threatening the woman with some weapon. But if she stayed, and he started shooting ... she waited, irresolute.

The man's voice was softer again, musing almost. 'I suppose you're thinking I killed the goose that laid the golden eggs. Just as well that there's Folly's cash to come, she's got enough for everything we'll need. Or she will have. But I wouldn't have had to do it at all if it hadn't been for you, Sarah. It's your fault, you deserve to suffer for it.'

'But why?'

'She said it was the last time, she was going to stop the money and tell her fool of a husband. She even talked about confessing to the police. Can you imagine it? I just had to do what I'd threatened, I had to get rid of her. I was forced to do it. Just because you'd talked to her, all those coffee sessions when you told her about your glamorous boy friend in London.' Incredibly, but briefly, complacency overlaid the anger in his tone. 'You let her know what the money was going on, the house, the car and all that. Not that she thought I should be celibate, Folly helped in the career prospects. But you didn't fit in the picture, you spoiled the way I was living up to my noble destiny.' For a horrible moment, as his voice sneered those words, Mrs White could visualize Margaret Knox saying them. She had a totally clear picture of how Margaret Knox must have loved amassing her ransom money to support the young man who had killed her.

'But then – Cherry?' Sarah Foster was keeping him talking, it was so obvious to the listeners outside that it was incredible that Victor did not realize it. PC Banting was edging closer to the door, his shoulders unconsciously braced.

'What do you mean? Who's Cherry?' he snapped.

'Cherry Millington. The baby. Was it a coincidence that she kidnapped her from me?'

'No, she knew all right, the damned fool. That was what was so unforgiveable. I'd told her I had to have that money, the bank was pressing me. Piles of bills, huge overdraft.

You do see, I had to have it? And then, when she left the cafe, there was that child, she always recognized babies when she had seen them once, and the mother had said there was a rich uncle. She thought it was *meant*, she said.'

'How did she do it?'

'Oh, what do I care about the bloody details? She worked some disguise trick with wigs, I think. What does it matter? She let me down and now you've let me down, there's nobody to trust in this world but myself —'

Some valedictory note in his voice must have come through. PC Banting burst the door open just as Victor's hand pressed the button on his aerosol tin, and Sarah screamed and flung herself on the floor. Vic was still staring stupidly at his non-functioning weapon when the policeman came beside him and twisted the container from his grasp.

Sarah squatted stupidly watching, trying not to be sick. Inappropriately, the pages of some long forgotten civics text book swam like a photographic negative between her eyes and the scene before her. The paragraphs had been headed in heavy black print and one had begun 'Members of Parliament: Immunity from arrest.' She watched as the policeman stood up, and followed by Victor close beside him, went through the door. Vic was holding his bandaged head high, and she averted her eyes as he passed; they rested on the the little yellow can which had held her terrified. Embossed on the bottom in tiny letters were the words 'Model only. Contains harmless volatiles.' She looked up again to see that the two men were crab-walking down the stairs. And she saw that the awkwardness of their gait was because their wrists were handcuffed together.

XX

Buddle, watching from a parked car in the main road, saw, in his wing mirror, the three sources of his income explode, their destruction symbolized by that almost invisible chain

146

which linked Victor Nightingale and the man in the summer suit.

He sat motionless, his hands lightly on the wheel. Was it his fault in some way? Could he have kept Vic going somehow, long enough to get at least the lump sum from Handles, if not the steadily increasing income he had counted on from Vic himself? He searched his own conscience and found it at fault. He could have postponed his glee at Vic coming unstuck, and been patient instead of being so eager to see that remote and impersonal face turn fearful and trapped. He couldn't see why his own actions should have had this disastrous effect. Even with the evidence before his eyes, nothing would make him believe that Victor had voluntarily handed himself over to the police.

But that was that, he accepted at once. No use in hoping that the money he had thought of as in his pocket would materialize now. At least there was no shortage of jobs for someone in his position. It ought to be easy enough to find one with somebody else about whom he could sell secrets. But what a waste of six months. Hardly anything to show for it at all. If only he hadn't been in such a hurry to wipe the smirk off his employer's face. That just showed what came of having emotions in this sort of profession.

Buddle's orders to come down here for the weekend had been left by Vic in a note on the hall table at the Chelsea house. He had been pretty angry that Vic had dared to tell him what to do, after the conversation they had had earlier in the day. He had thought, as he packed his gentleman's gentleman clothes, that the young man was going to try to brazen it out, continue his denials; he had said something about having a perfectly good alibi. Gordon Buddle had rather looked forward to wearing him down; it would have been quite entertaining to do so in the course of a stately home weekend, dropping hints as he ran the bath, making insinuations as he laid out the clothes, mentioning increasingly large sums of hush-money.

But the whole thing had been a let-down. This place wasn't even a stately home. One of the reasons that Buddle was still in his car was that he had been allotted a bed in the same room as one of the old man's nephews, a lean-to behind the kitchen of a drive gatehouse. Buddle wouldn't stand for anything like that.

Oh well, no use crying. At least he could have a good weekend in the Chelsea house. He started to run through a mental list of available chums. And that was when he suddenly realized that he might still cash in on this assignment. Not much use going for the woman in Orton; but he thought of Folly Armitage and licked his lips.

He went round to the boot of his car and took his suitcase from it. One could bear even a shared lean-to in a good cause.

He was sitting aimlessly in the kitchen of the lodge when Folly finally appeared for some ice. She had a large glass of whisky in her hand, and swigged it down when Buddle said he wanted to talk to her. She said,

'We'll go for a drive. No privacy round here.' They went out to Folly's car, a yolk yellow Mercedes, and she drove quite slowly off.

'We'll just go round the park, shall we?' she said, not waiting for an answer. The long bonnet swung in by a ticket booth, where notices announced that the driver was now entering a lion reserve; all windows to be kept closed, etcetera, etcetera. Buddle was not interested in animals, and hoped Folly would not expect enthusiasm from him.

On this day, when the rest of the park was devoted to the schools outing, the lion reserve was less full than it should have been on a fine summer afternoon. Some idle-looking lions lay in the shade under a group of trees, and as far as Buddle could see were no more worth looking at than dogs. Perhaps, he thought, they were dogs in disguise. Folly drove very slowly, winding through the reproduced veldt. She seemed to take as little notice as he of the wild life, merely changing gear to go over the cattle grids which divided the sections of the park. Buddle spoke insistently for some time. He had anticipated no difficulty in explaining what he wanted; the difficulty came in trying to make Folly realize her own position, and that, he found, was impossible.

148

She listened to his descriptions of her future reputation if Buddle told all he could tell, and she remained quite unmoved. Just laughed, in fact. In the end she said, quite kindly,

'You'll never persuade me to pay you to keep it dark that I slept with Vic. After all, everybody knows we went around together. They'd think I was pretty peculiar if I hadn't. What do a man and a girl do alone together, after all? You're old-fashioned, that's your trouble.'

'But the newspapers – if I sell the story?'

'Wonderful idea. Do,' she said cordially. 'Do sell it. I'm going to sell mine.'

'Your family?'

'Oh, pooh. You can't insult me or them with that. If you were to say I was no good in bed now – but you wouldn't know, would you? No, Gordon, you won't get any pay-out from me.'

Folly stopped the car in a kind of layby and stared at a group of animals which was just getting up from a recumbent position, and starting to pad restlessly about.

'Tame looking creatures, aren't they?' said Buddle, unimpressed.

She glanced at him with an expressionless face. 'I rather like them,' she said.

'Oh well, in that case.' He lit himself a cigarette, and wound down the window. 'Terribly hot, isn't it?' he said.

He leant back, eyes closed, and arm hanging out of the window. He was thinking that even if the girl wouldn't pay up, it was no use her thinking that she could turn him back into the impeccable manservant.

'What did you want to know about Vic's private life for, Gordon?' she said lightly. 'Just curiosity?'

'No,' he murmured, not opening his eyes. 'Handles Ltd. You must have heard of them.'

'Only vaguely. Tell me about it.'

'You must know. A lump sum for gen about anyone in public life. They're an agency really. You want a way of influencing so-and-so, they supply it. Very modern.'

'No use offering them one about me, so you tried me

direct, is that it?'

'That's right. Though I suppose if you'd married Victor Nightingale it would have been a different matter.'

'Really.' She allowed a silence to fall, after that one cold word. He puffed smoke out through his nose, determined to show her that he mattered. How could he prove it to this snooty bitch? Sitting there as though she was in judgment on him. He wouldn't have it. Buddle yawned and opened his eyes.

Folly was sitting still, her hands on the wheel, looking straight ahead.

'You'd really better let me have the cash,' he said. With one hand she turned the ignition on, with other pressed a button which sent his window whirring closed. His arm was trapped just above the elbow, and he said 'Hey!', and then, loudly and desperately, 'Hey quick, I'm caught – and look!' Half a dozen lions were padding towards the car, great yellow eyes fixed upon his waggling arm and fingers. One of them, looking absurdly cinematic, leapt roaring forward, and there was a shudder and thud as it landed on the roof of the car. At the same moment the window fell, and as Buddle slumped unconscious. Folly calmly pressed the button again to close it.

All the other parked cars nearby started to race their engines and hoot, and one of them, full of small children, accelerated past the Mercedes away from danger.

Folly watched calm-faced, as the creatures pressed against the car, rubbing curiously or greedily against the hot metal. When she saw a khaki Land Rover racing towards them she pushed her foot hard down on the accelerator, and the car jerked away, skidding on the hot dust.

Buddle was coming round, moaning and shuddering, his face revoltingly puce. Folly kept her eyes ahead, averted from the wreck of a man beside her. She smiled faintly as people came running to the car, when she stopped outside the double mesh fence. As streamlined a service as had been produced beside the model railway came into action, and a discreet brown ambulance took Buddle away. Folly had not looked at him again, and answered horrified questions with

150

an offputting calm. All she would say was that she had no idea the man would be such a fool as to open his window, what with all the notices there were forbidding it. But she had been in no danger herself. One of the men who had jumped from the Land Rover attracted slightly more of her attention than anyone else. He looked like a Hollywood white hunter, dressed in safari clothes and carrying a rifle. To him, Folly answered coldly, 'He deserved what he got. It won't be more than shock. The lion couldn't reach a vital part.' The man looked startled and refrained from asking the next question he had ready – which was why Folly had not used the electric window closing button before. She would not have told him, if he had. But she drove back to her uncle's house at a decorous speed, and did not think of the finished incident again.

XXI

Sarah was not as delighted by the return to normal life as she would have thought, considering how she had longed for it when surrounded by drama. She was still feeling off colour, and was pervaded by a feeling of humiliation, partly because her picture of herself, a year ago, would not have been of a woman who had love affairs, and partly because, the more she went over things in her mind, the more she realized that it was her own total self-absorption which had blinded her to the events going on around her. She should have realized, and anyone less selfish than herself would have realized, that there was something peculiar about Victor Nightingale's apparent wealth, about Margaret Knox's one-sided interest in Sarah, and about the fact that the fostered baby which Sarah had actually touched and cared for tallied so precisely with the descriptions of Karen Jones blazing from every headline. It was still an afterthought in her list of shames that she had betrayed Jeffrey; it was almost, she felt, as though his existence were so rock-like in her life, that it could be taken completely for granted; that none of the ridiculous tides which ebbed and flowed over him with his wife's vagaries would have the slightest effect.

Sarah's self-condemnation was not alleviated by a visit she had from Folly Armitage in her new role as 'girl reporter', noting down everything Sarah would say for the article she had sold in advance to a Sunday newspaper. Folly did not seem to mind it, but Sarah was almost speechless with embarrassment at the knowledge of what she and Folly had in common; and in a way it was galling that Folly, who had not been in the thick of the action, should now be in a position to explain the details of what had happened to Sarah. She had heard a good deal, it seemed, from her latest young man, the policeman called John Banting.

Vic, Sarah learnt, would plead guilty, which let them all out from giving evidence. He was expected to get about fifteen years, and with remissions for good behaviour, might be out in as few as ten. And he too, had sold his serial rights. That had been in the paper though, where Sarah had seen it, along with a leading article about criminal profits. She had had to resort again to the Children's Encyclopaedia, which had already shown her that Members of Parliament were immune from arrest only in civil matters, and was discouraged by what she read about the law of Libel and Slander. It didn't look as though forewarned would be forearmed against that.

Folly said that Buddle had told her a lot of the story, and that he had pinched the razor knife from the glove compartment of Vic's car and then handed it over to Folly because he did not want to be in possession of anything compromising. Sarah was shocked at the revelation of Buddle's second profession, but Folly described it unemotionally without mentioning how she had paid him out.

As for Margaret, it appeared that nobody missed her. Mr Knox had a readymade common-law wife and family waiting for him in London, and her only relation was a senile father who lived with his sister and her husband in a disused station near Orton. Her whole devotion had been

152

centred on her beloved cousin, and she had taken to her bizarre crime with the almost laudable motive of helping him to greatness. And Folly remarked complacently that there weren't many other profitable crimes a plain woman like that could have started on. It was not as though she would have been, for instance, a successful prostitute. Actually, upon a certain admiration for Margaret Knox's enterprise Sarah and Folly were agreed. Her scheme had been so elaborately organized that it deserved to succeed; and it was not as though the babies came to any harm.

From Buddle, Mrs White (who was dining out and broadcasting about her experiences with consummate self-satisfaction) and from John Banting, Folly had pieced together how Mrs Knox had planned her profession, for it was clear that she had intended to carry on subsidizing Vic with ransom money for years. Her system was to abduct the baby, which was only too easy for a respectable looking woman, to deliver it to her own house in her disguise as the official of a maternity home, and then to leave it in a drugged and silent sleep by dosing it with phenobarbitone, while she returned the van to the garage in Lodworth, changed back to her normal appearance, and came home in her own car. Returning the baby was equally easy, and the main problem would apparently have been the collection of ransom money, or of the expensive jewels which she would then turn into cash in jewellers shops all over the country. But even for this, there seemed to be enough relatively fool-proof methods to suffice for one woman's career. So long as the same person was not seen twice, and with modern methods of disguise she need not be, packages could be collected from any place where crowds of women milled; public lavatories, the mail pigeonholes in students' unions, hostels, airport bulletin boards and so on.

Folly left the moment Marcus and Emily came home, and Sarah only wished she could do the same. Domestic duties, far from being a welcome relief, seemed more onerous than ever. But she cooked Jeffrey an Escoffier style dinner that evening, and when she came back to the living-room, wiping her mouth and groaning Jeffrey said,

'When's it due?'

'February. How did you know?'

'When are you sick otherwise?'

'Are you pleased?'

Jeffrey got up and started leafing through the open volume which he had been studying before dinner. With his back to her he said,

'What's it got to do with me?'

She sat there goggle eyed, speechless. It was as though one of the tropical fish in the playroom had started to speak to her. She just wasn't used to Jeffrey talking to her, she realized suddenly. It was ages since he had. But she'd been so busy, her mind occupied . . .

'You must think I'm an awful fool,' he said lightly.

'Why, Jeffrey?'

'Producing a cuckoo for me. Suppose it has red hair or something? Hadn't you thought of that?'

'But —'

'I never saw him, as a matter of fact. What was his colouring? Do you think you might have got away with it?'

She lay back against the slippery sofa and smoothed her hair out of her eyes. She was sweating, and emotion was having its usual effect of turning her bowels to water. It made quite a change from feeling sick. She tightened her anal muscles, and belched absent mindedly. Her pregnancies had always been accompanied by the sound of her belching and she had ceased to notice herself doing it; but now Jeffrey hunched his shoulders and she could see he was disgusted.

'I'm out of the habit of you noticing me,' she said apologetically.

'Is that supposed to be an excuse?'

'No. But Jeffrey, about the baby, I assure you —'

'Please don't bother. It really doesn't matter to me.'

'But . . .'

'Look, Sarah.' He came and sat down in his usual chair, his face, as always, so mild and smooth that she could hardly believe that he was not teasing her. She pressed her hands against her bubbling stomach. 'It's useless for me now to start making protestations about how much I did love you. You might have had the perception to realize that just because I didn't talk about it all the time it didn't mean that I was bored by you. I never have been talkative, I never wanted to dissect our emotions when you had that psychology phase. I don't talk, I do things. But it doesn't mean that I'm a vegetable or something. What do you expect me to do when I find you've been having an affair with another man – criminal or not – and now you're pregnant?'

'But Jeffrey – you can't *know* that I slept with him.'

'Do you expect me to believe that?'

'I don't really see why not. How do you know about it all, anyway?'

'Oh, don't be a bore.'

Having, wantonly and carelessly, done everything in her power during the last few weeks to make it do so, Sarah was now astounded and hurt at the collapse of her everyday world. A bit of fun with Vic, a temporary irritation with Jeffrey, had not been intended to destroy the fabric of her life.

Jeffrey was sitting quite still opposite her, not smoking or doodling or making anything with his hands. It was almost the first time that she had seen him sitting thus unoccupied. He said slowly and tentatively, almost as if it embarrassed him to speak with such unprecedented introspection,

'You see, there must be so many different ways of loving. After all, poor Mrs Knox loved Victor Nightingale, and look how that ended up. Felicity Armitage loved him too; at least she seems to have been engaged to him. But it hasn't stopped her making a small fortune out of the end of their affair. And I've loved you, Sarah. Always, I loved having you there and living with you and knowing you were there at home with the children. You see, I thought you were happy too – oh, not on the surface. I know you're bored by housekeeping and looking after the kids, I know you kept yourself going in London by complaining to your little friends and telling them I never took you out. I suppose it's been difficult here. But I like Orton, I don't mind settling down here. Nice house, friendly people, a good job – I did not realize how determined you were to hate everything. But I've tried to be sympathetic to you. I gave you credit for being a little less silly than you were. I really thought we were doing OK. I was the more deceived.'

Sarah had once been told, by the English teacher at her school, that those five words of Ophelia's made the saddest sentence in the English language. She started crying, quietly but persistently.

Jeffrey got up and took down his model, and sat down with his glue and bits of cardboard. He had bought a new knife, a different make and different colour.

'Oh well, never mind, forget it,' he said. The overhead light was reflected in his bald head as he concentrated on his work. Sarah sobbed.

'You mean, you're just leaving it at that?'

'I don't really see what else I can do. But it won't ever be the same again.'

Sarah took out her knitting. It was a small white garment, half finished. She thought, butterfly fashion, about the last few months; they had moved to Orton and Emily had started at school and she had so much time to fritter. Wife-swapping parties and a glamorous lover, always with the certainty of a dull and faithful, but solid, reliable Jeffrey in the background, thinking she was marvellous. Abduction, death and murder trials; enough excitement to make a day of floor scrubbing seem restful. But if Jeffrey knew, what then?

'You're not walking out on me?'

'I don't feel bound to you, any more. You cut the knot. It'll be something for you to wait for, you can wonder whether every girl I meet at a party will be the one. I'm free again – as you were.'

He cut with a long firm slash on the thin cardboard; the next stage was the roof of the building. He turned on the wireless at his elbow, and after the last strokes of a clock, an impersonal voice said, in a list of other non-world shaking news, 'Mr Victor Nightingale, who is at present remanded in custody awaiting trial on a murder charge, was today appointed Her Majesty's Steward of the Chiltern Hundreds. Hundreds of football fans thronged the terraces as...'

'And now,' said Jeffrey, 'what about some tea?'